Metaphorosis

September 2022

Beautifully made speculative fiction

Also from Metaphorosis

Metaphorosis Magazine

Metaphorosis: Best of 20xx
Metaphorosis 20xx: The Complete Stories
annual issues, from 2016

Monthly issues

Plant Based Press

Best Vegan Science Fiction & Fantasy
annual issues, 2016-2020

from B. Morris Allen:
Chambers of the Heart: speculative stories
Susurrus
Allenthology: Volume I
Tocsin: and other stories
Start with Stones: collected stories
Metaphorosis: a collection of stories

Verdage

Reading 5X5 x3: Changes
Reading 5X5 x2: Duets
Score – an SFF symphony
Reading 5X5: Readers' Edition
Reading 5X5: Writers' Edition

Vestige

The Nocturnals, by Mariah Montoya

Metaphorosis

September 2022

edited by
B. Morris Allen

ISSN: 2573-136X (online)
ISBN: 978-1-64076-236-7 (e-book)
ISBN: 978-1-64076-237-4 (paperback)

Metaphorosis
a magazine of speculative fiction

from
Metaphorosis Publishing

Neskowin

September 2022

To the Wild Sea

B. Morris Allen

The tide seeped away, grey water into black sand. It left her lime-green boots uncovered, anomalous. *Just as well,* thought Sarosh, turning her back on the sea. *This planet could use some color.* As it had used Richard, used her dreams; swallowed them whole, and left nothing but little grains of sand that stuck to everything, fell off everywhere. She kicked the sand as she walked, and it spurted grudgingly before her feet.

At her back, the little love-lorn birds took up their plaintive cries, did their graceful runs and leapt ungainly into the air. 'Just what the planet needs,' she'd told him when he sent the first vid, 'moaning birds that can hardly fly.' He'd only laughed. 'I like it,' he'd said. 'It reminds me to be lonely.' She was lonely now.

Alira waved to her from the cabin above. Lonely, but not alone; no one with an assistant was ever truly alone. "What's up?" Sarosh asked, thumbing her net on.

'Listen,' he had said on their last virtmeet. 'The sea is calling me. Not telepathically, though.' She turned back to the surf, listened with one ear while Alira's voice poured schedules into the other. The waves crashed and stuttered and sighed across the sand in their alien language. "Richard," she told them. "Richard."

"Yes," said Alira from the porch, well clear of needy, sticky sand. "I just checked. There's nothing new in the search for him."

Sarosh walked back, kicked her boots against the foamcrete steps. He'd planned to cover them, he'd said, with native wood, or some equivalent. 'It's grass, really, but I can form it into planks.' She'd lost the rest of his comments, swirled them up with wind and sand and the sound of the sea.

"I'm sorry," said Alira for the hundredth time. She didn't like the beach, the way the sharp drop appeared at low tide and waves crashed fierce and furious at its rocky base. She risked a step down the stair, almost laid a tentative hand on Sarosh's shoulder. "Maybe tomorrow."

Maybe tomorrow, maybe the day after, the week after. All the maybe days rolled up in an endless bracelet of possibility and disappointment.

"Does this world have such a thing as months?" Sarosh asked. *This world*, because she refused to give it its romantic name, didn't care about the technical one.

"Yes, it does," said Alira, ever the perfect assistant, ever prepared. "Or it could. No one has named them yet. But with two moons, it could have a complex system of months." And who would have named them, if not Richard? Perhaps he'd done it. Perhaps up in the cabin, among his meticulous notes, was a native calendar, or in the scraps of poetry he'd left everywhere in his wake.

"How much longer can we stay?" Sarosh asked.

"As long as you want." Assistant as therapist, enabler.

I want to leave this place today and never come back. "How long?" she asked again. *I want to stay here, to bury myself in this cold black sand and wait and mourn and cry like a bird.*

"Ten days; local days. A thirtday if we have to. After that, there's the ... presentation to the grant committee." Alira hesitant because Sarosh and Richard had planned it together, this one little intersection of their professional worlds to match the intersection of their hearts. Begging for money she could have provided with a flick of her eyes.

"Send me the latest presentation," Sarosh said. "Whatever the home team has refined." Her crew would continue to update until the last minute, but it would not have changed substantially for thirts now.

"Of course. It's on your pad now." Professional tone hiding hurt that her boss could even hint she wasn't ready. It would be a new version after all, Sarosh realized. One with no role for Richard. The team would have taken his absence into account by now, might have had a Richard-less version waiting from the start. Just in case.

She looked up at the Richard-less cabin, climbed to its Richard-less porch, listened to the Richard-less voices of the birds.

"Are you alright?" She'd closed her eyes, like a child pretending that a thing she couldn't see was a thing she couldn't feel. An absence that couldn't touch her.

She opened her eyes, saw the concern in Alira's wide brown gaze. "I'm fine." She kicked sand off her boots where it had dried to a crust. "I'll work down the list for a while." There was always a list. Documents to be reviewed, expenses to be approved. All the things that came with a business spanning the width of a spiral arm. All the things that could be ignored and delegated. But not for long.

She sat on Richard's rickety grass-plank bench to take off her boots. Beyond the porch's protective screen, down by the dropoff, love-lorn birds raced to wrap prey in their wings. 'They're not mainly wings,' he had told her. 'It's how they eat. They fold these big flaps of skin around other creatures, and assimilate them.' Which he insisted wasn't just a poetic term for eating, that there was a transfer of knowledge. 'Like all the old myths of eating a creature to gain its skills.' But he'd been serious. She watched the birds' low bodies rise in staggered, wobbly surges, carrying borrowed knowledge up into rising wind. A storm coming; there was almost always a storm here, flinging sand against the screens, churning the sea into froth and ferocity.

"Alira. Gather up Richard's poetry." The scraps of scraps, scrawled words on crude paper he'd strewn like leaves across the house.

"It's in the box." The other woman stepped easily out of immaculate boots and into the immaculate slippers she'd left for them on the porch. "The blue stone one you gave him. I thought you might want it." The blue box of stone so light you could lift it with one finger, as if its carved floodbats were lifting it with cutout wings.

"Is there much?" She would go through it. That was her role, her contribution to his art; sifting through the leaves, helping him decide what to compost, what to keep; what had value. Tears started, and she looked to her boots. What had value. That was what she knew, what she saw. She had seen him.

"A few dozen fragments."

"It's not good, is it?" For a would-be telepath, he had been a terrible communicator. The tears seemed under control, and she slipped her feet into warm slippers.

"The poetry? Not really." Alira was honest, when she wasn't being supportive. It had been her main qualification for the job.

"No." The poetry had never been good. Even the pieces he'd written for her; especially those. Even the piece that had won her heart, back when her empire spanned only one planet, and he'd been an exo-biologist with a lunatic idea. The poetry had been treacly, dramatic, obvious. It had never changed. He had changed her, with his stupid, stupid words, and his follies. "I'll come later," she gasped, and held off the sobs until Alira had gone to the invisible, unobtrusive, ubiquitous world assistants went to.

Outside, a fog obscured the sea battering its way to the top of the dropoff with the rising tide. Not so much a fog as a spray, really, a haze as salty as the sea, and just as harsh. 'It's a bit alkaline,' he had

13

warned her, 'but beautiful. And full of life!' Because life was why he was here, why he had begged her to let him have this world for a threecent of days, unexploited, unexplored.

'I need to be the first,' he insisted. 'Before it's spoiled.'

'It's already spoiled, Richard.' It had had exobots crawling all over it, in their sterile, dragonfly bodies.

'You know what I mean. The first person. The first who thinks.' She had known, of course. Had known from their first meeting, when he said 'Hi. I'm Richard. I'm a telepath.' He'd never known what she was thinking, at that meeting, or the next, or the one that merged subtly into a date, then a relationship, then a life. He'd never known, and it hadn't mattered, because he knew what she felt, what she wanted and needed. 'That's not telepathy,' he'd scoffed. 'That's love.' As if there were a difference.

She looked out at the world she'd borrowed for him. A grey mist over black sand that hid love-lorn birds and sparklesing grass and slambang frogs and a hundred other strained names for strange creatures. A world borrowed from stockholders and creditors and staff who wondered why they weren't already exploiting the world and selling acreage and virt-safaris and phys-tours. All because of one man with conviction and a run of luck at esper card tricks.

And now he was gone. Vanished into howling winds, high seas, rocky coast. Vanished since just after their last talk, so that she'd only gotten the news when they climbed back down out of hype, already half the arm away.

Richard, she sent her call again. *Richard! Where are you?* On the beach, the sea rose, and the wind threw waves down on the hard sand, let them rise, threw them down again, again, again.

Richard. No answer came, and never would, because telepathy didn't exist. She'd told him as much at that first meeting, had laughed in his face, made a note to find out how he'd gotten past her assistant and her assistant's assistant. And, when he'd laughed back, brown eyes crinkling, short hair waggling, agreed to another meeting.

'There is no such thing as telepathy,' her assistant of the time had confirmed. All of them had. She'd had every new assistant look into it, even after she'd committed to spend her life with him, in

15

her mind, if not in words. 'They try to guess cards, tricks like that. Richard just got lucky.'

'Several times,' he'd pointed out. 'Consistently.'

'Coincidence,' she'd said. They'd all said. And he'd gotten his first grant from some tiny university with too big an endowment. In two three-cents of days, he'd failed to communicate with dogs, cats, birds, slugs, trees. With anyone but her. Even his funders seemed not to comprehend his failure. They'd kept funding him. And she'd kept seeing him, even as her business grew to other planets, to an entire system. Those had been good days, happy days.

She fell asleep in the little sitting room, woke to find herself stretched under a blanket on the sofa where no doubt Alira had arranged her limbs in the middle of the night. She fought her way muzzily to her feet and shuffled into her bedroom. Their room; Richard's room, and the reason she liked to forget to go to bed.

When she returned from the tiny shower, pH-adjusted, sterilized water dripping from damp hair onto a clean sweater, Alira had set out juice, cakes, a screen with tabs of news and business updates. She ate and read in silence while Alira sat in the kitchen, mumbling and tapping into her net.

"I'm ready," Sarosh said as she set down her empty juice glass. Alira came and smiled and took her seat on a hard chair opposite. Bright-eyed and bushy tailed and harder working than her boss. Sarosh had been the same once.

They spent the morning dealing with business until the list was tamed, pruned, manageable.

"I'll get lunch," Alira said, meaning she would choose from a dozen stat-packed gourmet meals an invisible staff prepared in the lander's kitchen, or brought down from the waiting ship above.

"Wait," Sarosh called. Alira turned, net ready, eyes bright. Tail bushy? What had she meant to say? "Bring me the poems."

"Of course." As if the blue box weren't visible on the little table across from the sofa, as if Sarosh were in the habit of being lazy.

"Thank you, Alira." She caught the younger woman's hand as it set the box down in front of her. She squeezed it gently, felt it squeeze back. "You're good to me." She let go, opened the box, tried not to see the brown eyes getting brighter as they turned away.

The box held scraps of hand-made paper, little squares and rectangles neatly smoothed and stacked. Richard would have left them crumpled all over the house. She had seen them, when they arrived, ignored them to focus on commanding exobots and overflights, search parties and radio calls, repeating every step her competent, loyal staff had already taken.

The fragments were just that, for the most part: little phrases and couplets in Richard's spiky scrawl.

A dog sat by the door of a house
And felt the shadows pass over him.
He waited in dark and light
While his master stayed inside.

Richard aiming for enigma.

Oh umbrous me, by an umbrose tree
How pleasant it is to be cool.

She chuckled. That was the other Richard — irreverent, funny, pointless. On a planet without trees.

Before a thickening twilight.

A fragment, destined never to carry more meaning than an awkward image. There were many more like it.

At the bottom, she found a slightly larger sheet, with what might have been a complete poem.

Give its due,
Its wrack and ruin.

Give your love
It cares nothing for.

To its spume and froth
Give your hopes
To the wild sea, the wild sea.

Dramatic, portentous, romantic. Richard through and through. The grammar was awkward. The second couplet didn't scan. She smoothed it against the table, let her tears fall upon its blue ink, let salt water smear the letters until they were gone. Then she folded it gently, put it back in the box and gathered the others in her hands for the recycler.

After a twenday, nothing changed. The moons raced and crawled across the sky, raised tides and storms, drained the sea to sharp rocks covered in flat, sheet-like fish with rubbery fringes, looking for something to envelop, to assimilate, to learn from. Richard had named them, no doubt, had made a note in his file for her scientists and marketers to consider.

'You just want to be Adam,' she'd accused, smiling.

'Come and be my Eve,' he'd said, though they both knew he wanted the world unsullied by other human minds. 'If I make contact, I want to be sure it's with aliens,' he'd joked before he left.

Naming had been a good use of his poetry. 'Get it out of your system,' she'd begged.

'I'm putting it in your system,' he'd said, though the company only owned the planet, had already sold the rights to the rocky inner worlds and the outer giants.

"Anything?" she asked Alira.

"I'm sorry." Torn between supportive and honest. "Nothing. It's been a tenday now," she anticipated.

Ten days with every available staff person landside, spending half their days thinking *Richard!*, and the other half listening. Waiting for signals from the only telepath in the entire arm. If there had ever been one.

"I thought," Alira was unusually hesitant. "I thought maybe someone who knew him."

Sarosh's jaw tensed. Did the fool think she hadn't tried? Hadn't spent her days and nights listening, calling, crying? Hadn't woken on her sofa to imagined calls that vanished as soon as she rose? But of course she knew. Alira had woken with her, brought her coats to wear in the storms outside, dried her off when she returned, fed her, clothed her, wiped her tears.

"I thought," Alira said, "maybe I would have more luck. Because I knew him better than the other staff did. More connection. But less invested, emotionally." Less likely to invent voices in the dark. "I didn't hear anything. I'm sorry. I ... I tried." Her dark eyes sparkled, and Sarosh saw the dark shadows that had pooled under them as Alira ran an empire single-handed while keeping its mistress warm and busy.

"I know you did, Alira. I know. I'm sorry too." She took Alira's soft hand and squeezed it, let it go as its owner hurried into the kitchen to let warm brown eyes spill into hot green tea.

"It's enough," Sarosh said as they sat later on the porch, red-eyed, warming their hands on Richard's thick ceramic mugs. Outside the barrier, the wind had calmed to a gentle breeze, the tide near its highwater mark. The love-lorn birds did their ponderous display flights, seducing mates with clumsy twists and dips.

"Are you sure?" Alira's voice was gentle. "We've stayed this long. I can put everything off until the grant presentation."

"No." And she would go through with the presentation, would not fund it herself, because that was what Richard would have wanted. And if they got the grant, would send some young fool out here to listen for alien voices in his mind. And any others he heard. "No, it's enough. We'll go to Alteph, then Likun. That will leave us close enough to Ghenna that we can present in person rather than virt." She looked out at the black beach again. "Pack. Let me know when the lander is ready."

"Of course." A tentative hand settled on her arm, vanished.

She slid the slippers off her feet, slid into lime-green boots. Outside the screen, the wind was warm, freighted with foreign messengers of scent and salt. She let it blow her toward the water. The love-lorn birds squealed and raced on delicate legs to rest a few meters away. They moaned their sad moan, calling for mates already beside them, and every now and then flapping unwieldy wings to lift slowly into the wind.

The sea sputtered and spat and sent its feelers out and back, out and back in slow, bubbled waves. She squatted at its edge and took a folded paper from her pocket.

"Here," she said, letting the poem settle into the water. "My wrack and ruin. My love." The caustic water soaked the paper, bled the ink away in little blue swirls. An undertow sucked black sand grains over the top. "That's enough. My hopes I'm keeping." She stood and turned away to wave at Alira, waiting patiently at the top of ugly foamcrete steps. Behind her, the soft, assimilating swish of the sea called her name.

See B. Morris Allen's story "To the Wild Sea"
online at Metaphorosis.
If you liked it, leave a comment. Authors love
that!
Remember to subscribe to our e-mail updates so
you'll know when new stories are posted.

About the story

I woke up one morning with the whole central poem in my head, drawn from a dream I couldn't remember, except that it had something to do with telepathy. While flawed, the poem was so clear that I wanted to do something with it, and I formed the story around it. While it's subtle, it's important to note that the world it takes place on is all about assimilation. Sarosh's husband may not be quite as completely vanished as it seems. Unfortunately, she doesn't seem to notice.

For the Love of Wild Things

Mande Matthews

It started the day she returned from the morgue. Mrs. Ruddle Wildemore was sliding the key into the door lock when something moved at the edge of her sight.

She glanced into their—correction, *her*—forest garden. A suncatcher swayed from a branch, casting rainbows on leaves, berries, and bark. Its brass bell *ting... ting... tinged...* in the summer breeze. Tangerine nasturtiums peppered black earth—those had been Rudy's favorite salad topping—and beyond, sixty-year-old branches hung down like familiar hands. The walnut tree had been the first Rudy planted when they moved to their

Trout River homestead, once a sapling, now a towering giant, the center from which their wild garden sprang.

No. *Her* wild garden. Could she ever think of it as just hers?

Willamina's gaze settled on the old trunk. Her sight wasn't what it had been in her twenties, or even in her seventies, for that matter. She'd thought she saw something materialize and scurry up the tree. Had she seen anything at all? Had it been a squirrel? It hadn't looked anything like a squirrel. Or a bird. Or a rabbit...but then, rabbits didn't climb trees.

"Hello? Is anyone there?"

The sleeves of her linen blouse fluttered with the wind's touch, tickling her crepey skin. When nothing but the leaves and petals shifted, she whispered, "Rudy? Is that you?"

The sun's warmth rested on Willamina's thinning hair, tied back in a structured bun. The color of her hair, stark white, bore no remembrance of what it once had been.

Willamina tried to recall Rudy's face, but the memories surfacing were ones she didn't want to see. She wanted him vibrant and young. Planting berry bushes, dirt-caked in his nail beds, a trowel tucked through the loop of his coveralls, but those memories were fragments at the edge of her sight. And the others? The ones that were brash and blaring and insistent? She refused them. Or at least, she tried.

"Rudy?" she asked again but of course, nothing replied. Certainly not Rudy.

Willamina knew that whatever she thought she had seen could not be him, so she turned the key and entered her empty house.

"Rudy, I'm home," Willamina called, not because she thought he would answer but out of a sixty-year-old habit.

Willamina Wildemore's house was more organized than a library. She might as well have card-cataloged each item. It hadn't always been so. Not when Rudy was younger and well and impossible to contain. His wildlife rescues had once ruled their domain, turning Willamina's attempts at orderliness into a zoo: injured raccoons raiding cupboards, a white-tail deer hoofing over her oak floors, squirrels hanging from the pinewood ceiling beams, and once, a three-legged bear in her well-labeled, alphabetized pantry.

There had been days she'd cried over the chaos, but now the noiselessness of her home hurt like the aftermath of an explosion when all the debris had settled, when the broken parts lay exposed, when the silence of the destruction wormed into her bones.

It nearly brought Willamina to her knees, but she was a rational woman. She'd been the one to hold the pieces together while Rudy, quiet as a storm on the horizon and as wild as nature, built his outlandish dreams into reality—the ones everyone had warned him against.

Even Willamina's mother, when she was alive, had bent her daughter's ear too many times about such nonsense. "Why can't that man get a job in town with a good pension plan? Who wants to grow their food when you can buy it in a can, ready to heat and eat? Why on God's green earth do you have to live in the middle of nowhere? Don't you want a comfortable life? Pretty dresses? A washer and dryer? A television? Twinkies for breakfast and Little Debbie's for dessert?" And when her mother was more exasperated by their seeming lack of progress—an entire year spent building compost piles and living in a tent, she'd complain, "The country is moving forward, and that man insists on living like a heathen foraging for berries and mushrooms. I swear to Jesus and Mother Mary, Willamina, if I come for a visit and that man's wearing nothing but a loincloth, I'll drag your father here with a shotgun to take you home and marry you off to an accountant or doctor! Someone that can provide for you right and proper!"

No one had heard of food forests in the 1960s. Most certainly not Willamina's parents. When the world was pushing pesticides, modified crops, and convenient contraptions like microwaves to speed up meal preparation, Rudy had cultivated the contrary.

Besides, it didn't matter. There was no telling Rudy what could and could not be done.

Now, standing on the threshold to her living room—where herbs grew from hanging pots, where recovering robins had once perched on branches screwed into the walls, where she and Rudy had shared their lives—Willamina knew nothing could turn back time. Wishing for what's gone was for dreamers. Rudy had been the dreamer. Not her.

She dialed the *Trout River Gazette* on her rotary phone and asked to speak to the person that could place an obituary.

"How much?" Willamina asked.

"Starts at two hundred and fifty dollars, ma'am, but can run you up to five hundred if you want to include a picture."

That was over a quarter of her social security payment. Though they had mainly lived off the homestead, Rudy had worked at the Fish and Wildlife Service for supplemental income which ended up providing a modest retirement. But with Rudy's final costs and the medical bills...

Tears pushed at her eyelids. The cuckoo clock *click, click, clicked* into the stillness.

"You there, ma'am?"

"I'll let you know," and Willamina replaced the handset onto the base.

She sat on the log couch Rudy made some fifty years ago. Even though the place was filled with the essence of Rudy —the walls and foundation around her constructed with his own hands, sweat, and sometimes blood, the furniture he made from fallen logs and twisted willow branches—it didn't bring back the memories she longed for. It only made her feel his absence more, like a fire poker in an open wound.

A breeze wafted in, like a huff of breath, even though no windows were open. A *clack* followed, and Willamina spotted a toppled photo frame. *Odd.* She picked it up, and any hint of wind disappeared.

In their faded 1960s wedding picture, Willamina was twenty, yarrow-laced hair trailing to her waist. Rudy was thirty-one, with owl-rimmed glasses and an uncombed beard to his chest. They held hands beneath a grapevine arbor constructed on their barren plot, gazing into each other's eyes, ready to conquer the world together.

They looked like strangers to her now.

Passing at ninety-one, Ruddle Earnest Wildemore had outlived his brothers and sisters by over a decade. And as the youngest (some called her an afterthought) of three, so had Willamina. The couple was childless, grandchildless. All their old friends had passed. Nieces and nephews scattered all over the country had long since lost touch.

Now, it seemed, Rudy would die without notice. Drift away without anyone to celebrate his accomplishments. Not only was a memorial too expensive, but there wasn't anyone left to attend.

He had been a kind man, full of tenderness and dedication. He didn't deserve to go unseen. In Willamina's estimation, he'd been overlooked for his good work his entire life—thought of as a crazy old forest fool.

Willamina would have drowned in those thoughts had it not been for the sharp whistle blasting from the kitchen.

Two western harvest mice stood by a steaming cup of chamomile tea, and, it seemed, another was busy turning off the burner where the wailing teapot sat. The critter leaped from the butcher block countertop, caught hold of the temperature dial, swung until the knob turned to OFF, vaulted to the floor with one Olympic-style mid-air somersault, landed, and skittered away.

Willamina wagged her jaw as if to say something, but what could she say? Mice had gotten the tea, the kettle, and the cup from the cupboard and brewed tea.

How could mice even carry a teacup, let alone a kettle?

It was absolute, utter nonsense.

Still, the fragrance of chamomile drifted to her. Rudy had been the one to make it for her with flowers picked out of their garden whenever her nerves were frazzled, which had been often in their earlier years together.

Later, he'd brought it to her every morning when she'd gone through the change and any last hope of a child of her own faded. She'd wondered if he'd filled the house with his rowdy rescues to keep her from that sadness. That loneliness of being childless. Of knowing this day would come—the day when no one but her would be left.

But Willamina didn't remember any of that now. Those memories were blocked behind a gauzy curtain that could not be pulled aside. She only remembered there was something comforting about the chamomile. Something that gave her pause. Something that she should remember.

One of the mice turned its little bottom to the teacup and pressed into it. A puff of air ruffled its fur, and it nudged the cup in her direction. Which was, by all accounts, impossible. The mouse couldn't have weighed a tenth of the full teacup. And yet, the cup slid toward her as if moved along by an invisible hand.

Rudy would have said, "Look, Willa! The elementals are here. Do you see them?" And Willa would have snorted, rolled her eyes, and said she saw no such thing.

But of course, Willa didn't recall any such conversations.

The second mouse stood on its hind legs, shiny eyes imploring. The third squeaked a chorus of nonsensical mouse-talk.

A flutter of movement caught her eye, and that was when Mrs. Wildemore noticed the row of birds landing on the windowsill: a bushtit, a dark-eyed junco, a white-crowned sparrow, and even a dove joined and cooed.

Not knowing what else to do, she picked up the cup and sipped. She swore the mouse on its hindlegs nodded in approval.

The liquid settled the knot she'd held inside since she'd found Rudy dead in their bed.

Unlike the faded memories she couldn't capture, this one was a technicolor movie on loop. Willamina had snuck beneath her dead husband's arm and huddled against his chest like a frightened child, hoping that he hadn't left her. That he was sleeping. Just sleeping. He'd awaken and tell her he loved her. That he'd never leave her. That they'd always be together.

The sticky quills of Rudy's feather pillow had poked her shoulder. "Please don't go. I can't live without you," she'd whispered to his cold corpse.

A chorus of birdsong had played outside the window as if nothing had happened, repeating like a broken record: *chirp, chirp, chirp, twitter, trill... chirp, chirp, chirp, twitter, trill.*

The room had seemed icy, like Rudy's skin. She didn't want that memory.

As the tea settled in her stomach, another memory crossed Willamina's mind. Nothing bright or brilliant like the last. No. This memory was like flipping through an old scrapbook, the pages going by too quickly to make out much. A picture here. A word scribbled there. A newspaper clip glued to a page. But a memory it was. And it went something like this:

Rudy. Nursing a hare. A snowshoe? A jackrabbit? It had been mauled. By a cougar? A bobcat? A coyote? It lay on Rudy's lap, dying.

Willamina sat next to him. Holding his hand? Or was her hand on his shoulder? The hare, or rabbit, convulsed one last time and lay lifeless.

Rudy said, or she thought he said, "Did you feel that?"

"Feel what?"

"His spirit cross. His energy rise up and out and all over. Uncontained. Free. Joining the nature spirits."

Nature spirits, or elementals, were what Rudy called fairies. That, Willamina could not forget. She had never believed in them, but Rudy did. Said they were everywhere. Said you felt them. Said you could see them if you were open. That the world, this big beautiful dance of energy, had many secrets hiding in plain sight if one would just look.

"I felt nothing," Willamina had said.

At least, she thought she had said so then.

Now, she sat sipping tea with three mice and a flock of birds in the kitchen Rudy had built. The implausibility of the situation and the implications of her state of mind unsettled her. Deciding it was time for no more nonsense, she left the kitchen without so much as a glance at the critters.

"Cremation or burial?" the funeral home director asked, bifocals balancing on the tip of his nose. He stared at the form, all questions and checkboxes, a ballpoint pen ready in hand.

"Cremation," Willamina said.

"Are you sure you don't want a burial? There are nice plots at Peaceful Rest Cemetery for only $3,555. What about the service? We have a full-service funeral package for $7,649.95, including the coffin, unless you want to upgrade. Of course, if you choose cremation the coffin will be cremated along with your loved one. But it's worth the investment. Our solid mahogany model is lined with high-quality velvet and makes a beautiful final presentation."

"No service," she said. "We want a cardboard casket. And I have the urn he chose here." Willamina sat the box she'd been holding on the funeral director's desk. It was a simple biodegradable urn that the palliative care counselor helped them purchase after his diagnosis had been confirmed.

"I see." The director fixated on her, sliding his bifocals down. "If you don't mind me asking, you're on a fixed income, right?"

Willamina nodded.

"And my paperwork says you live out on Old River Road, is that correct?"

"Yes."

"By yourself?"

"With Rudy."

"I see."

He removed his glasses and scrubbed at his eyes. A plastic ivy trailed off the bookshelf behind him. There weren't books on the shelves, but coffin catalogs, headstone flyers, urns, and one very peculiar necklace with a pendant made of swirling colors. A sign next to it read:

> *Always have your loved one close to your heart. Create a one-of-a-kind keepsake with their ashes to hand down to your children and grandchildren. 24-karat gold chain and bail. Starting at only $595.*

Mrs. Wildemore thought the director might present cheaper options, but he led Willamina into the viewing room to see Rudy one last time instead.

Rudy's naked body was covered with a sanitary hospital sheet and laid out on a metal gurney. Willamina tugged at his soft beard. Someone had brushed it out, taken away all his unruly curls. She kissed his waxy lips, but there were no words she could muster for goodbyes. This. This man lying lifeless. This was not Rudy. Not her husband. Not her love. It just… couldn't be.

When Willamina puttered up Old River Road in her '72 Chevy LUV pickup, a raccoon saluted her. It raised on its hind legs, looked directly at her, or so she thought, lifted its short arm in the air, and waved its long fingers in front of its forehead in a military manner. Willamina blinked.

It couldn't be.

I'm tired. Just tired.

At least, that's what she told herself.

Once inside, Willamina smelled something coming from the kitchen.

Something pleasantly scented. Delicious, even.

When she entered the kitchen, she noted the mice had taken up residence in the pantry. When Rudy became ill, Willamina had set about canning all she could. She knew there would be no line of mourners with casseroles at her doorstep, no baskets of cookies and condolences. Consequently, her pantry was jam-packed.

Mice hopped from mason jar to mason jar. They squeaked back mouse-ish to another, who looked, beyond all comprehension, to be taking inventory—counting on little mouse fingers. Could that be right?

But that activity wasn't the most curious part.

A saucepan sat on the stovetop. A china bowl from her Summer Roses set, which her mother had given them as a wedding gift, sat on the table over a crocheted tablecloth alongside a spoon and wafers.

Willamina stirred the concoction and tasted it. Just a dab on the end of the ladle.

Cream of asparagus soup. Rudy's favorite.

A flash of images: Rudy. In the garden. On his knees, trowel in one hand, asparagus bunch in the other, grinning up at her. He said, "Here's looking at you, kid." But as quickly as it came, the memory left. Gone. Replaced with nothing but the desire for more. She dropped the ladle into the saucepan.

Mrs. Wildemore had had about enough. She tossed the spoon and bowl into the sink. A sickening crack sounded as porcelain met porcelain, making her angrier.

She picked up a broom and swatted at the mice. "That's enough! Enough! Enough!"

The little critters went scurrying across the oak floor.

Willamina couldn't bring herself to sleep in their bed. Not this soon after. She hadn't even had the strength to change the bedding. So she walked into the forest garden.

As she crossed under the grapevine-laden arbor, the same one she and Rudy exchanged vows under, it seemed odd she'd mourn Rudy's death in late summer, when everything around her was so alive.

Deep purple huckleberries spotted green leaves. Chamomile, white petals surrounding cheery yellow heads, bloomed in patches of sunlight. Crimson stems peeked from under umbrella-like rhubarb leaves. Water babbled in the background where the creek met the Little Trout River. And the scent. Forest pine, sweet wildflowers, and honeysuckle mixed in an intoxicating way. The smell was unlike any other. It smelled like home. It smelled like Rudy.

Rudy's master plan had been to return the scarred earth to a natural state of abundance, and the walnut tree had started it all. He had called it a food forest and said it was how people were intended to live—in harmony and cooperation with nature—and that someday people would recognize that wisdom. Maybe after he was gone, perhaps after they both were, but eventually, people would have to see it if the world was to survive.

Willamina sat down beneath the tree, arranging her tea-stained skirt. Feather moss cushioned her bony bottom. She rested her back against the scaley trunk and closed her eyes.

Mr. Wildemore had brought his blushing bride to the Little Trout River in the wilds of Washington State in 1962. He'd tugged Willamina out of the passenger's side of his Ford pickup, coaxed her to the center of a naked twenty-acre plot, and gestured as if presenting treasure to a queen.

The land was a scar within the over-logged forest. Loggers had used the spot for decades, dragging felled trees into the river to float them downstream to the mill, scraping up topsoil trip after trip, year after year, decade after decade, until nothing grew back and the ground beneath was barren. Lifeless. Not soil, but nutrient-depleted dirt. There wasn't a bird to be heard. Or a rabbit in the bush. There weren't even any bushes! Everything around them was dead.

Rudy waited, watching his bride from behind his owl-eyed glasses. He wore that cockamamie half-grin, one side up and the other down. His bushy eyebrows matched his sideways smile in their crookedness. His bellbottoms settled in the dirt like he was dug in, growing roots with his heels. The gush and splash of the

Little Trout River sounded behind them as moments frittered away.

"No." Willamina planted her hands on her hips, a gesture which was as solid as Rudy's heels in the ground. "We won't be able to grow a garden here."

Rudy swept his arms around again as if she hadn't seen its majesty the first time.

"No, Rudy. We're miles from town. I will not live without electricity."

"There's a pole a few miles back down the road." The sky rumbled above them like an orchestra tuning before a performance. The scent of rain filled the air.

"I will not live without running water."

"I'll pump from the river."

"This is not the 1890s, Ruddle Earnest Wildemore."

"Hey, now. Don't sweat it, baby girl. We'll even have a telephone. Cross my heart. I'm gonna take good care of you. You know that, right?"

"Yes, but—"

Rudy pulled her into him. Tugged her defiant hands off her hips. Circled them around his waist. Hugged her tight and kissed her. Sprinkles plopped down on their exposed noses and cheeks, but the two kept at their kisses, lost in one another's touch, until Willamina remembered her mission. She pulled out of his hug.

"Rudy, I'm serious. I—"

A *kee-eeeee-arr* sounded above them.

They looked skyward as a red-tailed hawk circled, coming lower and lower until it landed in the dirt not two feet from them. It hopped over and dropped a long-bearded hawkweed at their feet. The hawk cocked its head and stared.

Rudy raised his eyebrows at Willamina.

"It means nothing," said Willamina.

"It's a sign," said Rudy.

"It's not a sign."

"Then what is it?"

Willamina couldn't deny the oddity of the moment, even though she'd become accustomed to peculiar happenings around Rudy. It seemed that Rudy was connected to something mystical but whenever Willamina had such a thought about him, she dismissed it. Nothing could convince her life was not a practical matter to be handled sensibly.

Rudy grasped both of her hands. "We're meant to restore this land. Build a food forest. Bring back nature. Feed the wild things. Live in harmony. I feel it in my bones, Willa. The natural things want this. They're telling us to do this." Indeed, the hawk kept staring at the newlyweds as if it agreed. "It's my purpose."

But was it Willamina's? "Look at this place. Everything's dead."

"Oh, baby doll. Close your eyes," he said, "and imagine."

"No, Rudy. We need to be rational."

He turned her around and put his palms over her eyes.

"Oh, Rudy, stop." But she laughed at his touch.

"Just keep your eyes closed." He leaned close. He wound his arms around her stomach, tugging her into the comfortable curve of his body.

Willamina opened an eye, and he scolded, "No peeking."

She giggled like a schoolgirl but complied.

"I wish you could see what I see. The magic. The majesty. The possibility." The seriousness of his voice stilled her. She listened. Listened with all her body. "It's alive. Nature is all around us. Waiting for us. Waiting for our vision. Our hands. Our work. See, there's a walnut tree in its prime, bearing hundreds of pounds of nuts, at the center of our wild forest garden. Our house is not fifty steps away, built with naturally fallen pine. Berries, chestnut trees, rhubarb, and mushrooms are ready for harvest for months out of the year. Squirrels and birds, foxes and field mice, raccoons and whitetails return, and our forest garden feeds not only us but them. Nature is allowed to be nature again. Can you see it? There in your mind's eye? Can you see what we can create?"

Willamina wanted to. Wanted it with all her heart. But then she opened her eyes to the scarred earth, to the abuse that seemed irreversible. "Nothing lives here, Rudy."

He grinned again. Though she couldn't see it, she felt it, and knew he wore that troublemaking smile. "*Au contraire*, Madame Wildemore. *We* do. And with a bit of elbow grease, so will an entire forest of living things."

The hawk beaked the flower and tossed it toward them. It landed on the toe of Willamina's Mary Jane, a yellow splash on black. Then the hawk took to the sky with a *whoop, whoop, whoop* of his wings.

"You can't argue with that," said Rudy.

"You're irrepressible."

"And that's why you love me," he said.

It was true. She loved him more than she'd loved anything in her young life. She loved him because of the wonder she saw behind those owl-round eyes. She loved him because he saw worlds more beautiful than what existed before them. She loved him because the word 'impossible' was only a catalyst for change for him. Rudy held more belief in his little pinky finger than anyone she knew, especially her. In that way, she supposed, they balanced out. Complemented each other. He, the dreamer, she, the rationalist. She might not have believed nature was alive and incarnate, but she believed in Rudy. And if he believed, she'd support him one thousand percent.

"Do you have any idea how much I love you, Mr. Ruddle Earnest Wildemore?"

"Not more than I love you, my gorgeous, big-hearted wife." Rudy picked her up as he'd done on their wedding night, cradled her to his chest, his beard tickling her cheek. He spun her in circles beneath summer rain clouds, the hawk circling above them. Sprinkles turned to a downpour, a musical *pitter-patter* like a band at a country dance, and Willamina's squeals turned to laughter, and Rudy's smiles turned to kisses, hungry and passionate.

But that's not what Willamina remembered. The memories had faded, turning to mush—blotted pictures in her head, watered-down words in her ears. And now, more than ever, she wished to recall it.

But everything about that day was a blur. Remembering how barren the land had been was near impossible. Even though her wedding photos gave glimpses of the homestead before Rudy's decades of dedication, the entirety of the land's disfigurement was lost to her.

But she remembered the hawk. Was it a hawk? Or an eagle? She remembered the flower. Was it a yellow hawkweed or a purple lupine? Maybe a white, daisy-like phlox?

Had a hawk dropped a flower at their feet? Or had she made up the memory to comfort herself?

What Willamina *could* remember were those last months: Rudy, declining, the life sucked out of his sunken cheeks, the trips to the Saint Paul's hospital, waiting for hours in antiseptic rooms, the news of stage four melanoma metastasized to the lungs, the doctor's deadpan face when he delivered his "only a few months" prognosis, then finding her love dead in their bed.

Willamina wished those memories would fade and the other wild-about-life Rudy memories would return.

A puff of air caressed her cheek, and a curious thing happened when Willamina opened her eyes. She found a bright yellow, long-bearded hawkweed lying on her lap.

Not a day later, someone knocked on the door. Willamina couldn't imagine a single soul who would drop by, and when she opened the door, no one was there. She stared into her wild garden, expecting movement like the day she had returned home from the morgue.

The breeze pushed up the fishy scent of the Little Trout River. Nothing moved, but when Willamina thought to close the door, she heard something chatter.

There, not a foot away from the door's threshold sat a red squirrel. Its shiny eyes looked up at her; rusty-red ears twitched. It held a blueberry out to her in one of its paws.

"Oh, no," she said. "No more of this imaginary nonsense," and she started to shut the door.

"*Rah...Rah...Rah...*" cried the squirrel. Its whiskers twitched. It blinked. It held up the arm not bearing the blueberry, and that's when Willamina realized its wrist hung like a floppy noodle.

Then Willamina said, "Rudy." It wasn't because she didn't remember Rudy was gone but because rescue was Rudy's love. His passion. His mission, along with the restoration of the land. Yes, she'd assisted him, but Rudy, always Rudy, did the mending.

So she said his name like a prayer, and it was for Rudy's sake she asked the squirrel, "What happened to you?"

The critter chattered away like it was explaining.

And despite Willamina's rational judgment, she stepped aside and waved it in.

It scurried across the floor, holding up its injured foreleg, scrambled into the kitchen, scaled the tablecloth, and sat waiting for Willamina.

If she had imagined the mice and tea... If she had concocted the nut cream of asparagus soup... If the raccoon salute was merely a mis-seeing of what happened... If the hawkweed just blew in on the breeze and coincidentally settled in her lap... All those things had happened or not. But the critter on her kitchen table required attention. If she proclaimed it fiction and turned it away and it wasn't, then what?

What would Rudy do? What would Rudy *want her* to do? And for that matter, what did Willamina want to do? Hadn't she done this for the better part of her life, too?

But nothing came to mind.

Willamina looked for supplies. Herbs for pain? For calming? What to use, what to use? Didn't Rudy keep a medical emergency bag?

When she turned back to the squirrel, two mice had joined the patient on the table. One balanced atop an isopropyl alcohol bottle, another held a popsicle stick with its forepaws, and a bandage ball rolled across the table by itself.

A blue jay landed, offering her a cotton ball. It seemed the logical next move, so she wetted it with alcohol. The red squirrel stretched out its limp hand and covered its eyes with the other.

But when it came to the moment of doctoring, Willamina wasn't sure what to do. Yes, she'd fetched the supplies, boiled tea, and made poultices, which she vaguely remembered. Still, Rudy, always Rudy, knew what to look for, how to test for fractures, clean wounds, make splints, and administer liquids, sub-Q or through a syringe or a bottle or...

Willamina closed her eyes, willing Rudy's guidance. But just because she wished for him didn't mean he would come.

She sighed, took a breath, and fumbled through it. She blotted an open wound. Then cut the sticks into tiny splints and wrapped the little paw with the bandage. The result was not Rudy's caliber, though she couldn't quite remember what standard Rudy had held. But it would, perhaps, do the job.

When Mrs. Wildemore looked up from her work, she realized an audience had gathered in the kitchen. A woodrat, a pocket gopher, and a yellow-bellied marmot lined up. Even a mule deer fawn stood on unsteady legs.

But they weren't just spectators. Upon inspection, each bore some wound that needed tending.

Mrs. Wildemore set out to help them, but she dropped the bottle of alcohol on the floor, resulting in an antiseptic puddle. The bandage slipped from her hand and rolled underneath the cupboard. She slipped on the wet floor and cracked her head on the table when she tried to fish it out.

She sat on her haunches, held her head with her hand, and willed, *willed!* Rudy's memory to her. *Show me what to do.* She tried to remember him. Were his hands capable or gentle or both? Were his eyes intelligent or compassionate or both? Were his actions quick like a snake's strike? Or soft like a doe's nuzzle? This was Rudy's domain. Not hers. He was the one who worked at Fish and Wildlife. The one with a degree in biology. The one who had trained as a wildlife emergency caretaker. Rudy was the forest mastermind. The magic healer. The spiritual shaman.

And she was...what?

The memories wouldn't come. Just the overwhelming proof of her insufficiency and the lack of his presence.

"Rudy, why did you leave me?"

The red squirrel *chucked* and inched toward her, but she held out a hand to stop it.

"I can't," she said. This was Rudy's dream. Rudy's skill. Rudy's compassion. And he wasn't there anymore. So Willamina said, "Get out."

The animals pressed in around her.

"Get out! Get out!" she yelled.

The animals bowed their heads, filed out the door, and disappeared into Rudy's forest garden.

After they'd gone, including a moose who had stood behind a western larch and grunted when she shut the door on him, their wedding photo fell over, frame first, onto the coffee table. Willamina picked it up, clutching it to her chest.

"Oh, Rudy."

She lay on the sofa, curled her legs as far as the old fragile things would bend, and did something she had not allowed herself to do. Something she'd thought if she started, she'd never stop.

She cried. Sobbed. Wailed for the loss of Rudy. His absence. Her loneliness. The pain it caused in every bone of her body.

For how much she missed him. For being left behind. For how she'd never be with him again.

As she did, the wind howled outside. It shook branches and limbs, bushes and grasses. It banged on the shutters. The dark sky poured droplets as large as treefrogs and drummed against the rooftop. Lightning crackled like anguished gods.

Critters of all species pressed wet noses to the windowpanes: a Rocky Mountain elk, a California bighorn, more squirrels and raccoons and birds and rats, and even a cougar, prey and predator at peace for the moment. They joined the storm and watched the grieving woman, somber as pallbearers.

Later, reports would confirm a power outage happened at that exact moment.

But Willamina knew nothing of all that. For all she knew, there on the couch, eyes blurred with tears, snot running, chest squeezing, she wept alone.

Rudy's face appeared out of the blackness, wiry beard dangling to his flannel pockets, earth-brown eyes behind

owl-eyed   glasses.   Intent.   Serious.
Compelling. Lights danced around his
head like translucent feathers. He was
vibrant and young and oh, so beautiful.
He reached for Willamina, hands stained
with rich black earth.

"You can see what I see, Willa. You
can. Just open your eyes."

A knock at the door startled Willamina
awake.

Rudy. Rudy. Rudy!

But he'd gone. Willamina refused to
open her eyes. If she kept them closed,
he'd return. She could continue the
dream. Continue being with him. At least,
she hoped that would happen.

Knock, knock, knock.

"Mrs. Wildemore?" called a nasal voice.
"Are you home? Hello?"

Go away, said Willamina in her head.
She hadn't the strength to bring the words
to her lips. She wanted to return to Rudy's
dream.

"I'm Laura Doyle from Adult Protective
Services. I'm delivering your late
husband's ashes from the Peaceful
Slumber Funeral Home. Are you there?"

Maybe the intruder would leave if Willamina stayed still, curled on Rudy's couch, the sun through the window warming her eyelids. But it occurred to Willamina that a social worker delivering Rudy's ashes wasn't good. It must have been why the funeral director had been so inquisitive about her finances—to assume incompetence and rally the authorities to do a home check. It wasn't the first time she'd been treated as incapable because of her age, or where and how she lived. Small towns were infamous for neighborhood busybodies; Trout River wasn't exempt, and *that* was enough to rouse her.

"I'm coming," said Mrs. Wildemore and rallied herself to open the door.

"Hello. I'm Laura Doyle. It's nice to meet you." She held one plump hand out for a shake while cradling Rudy's urn.

The cuckoo clock *tik toked*. Laura wore a collared shirt and a rhinestone fleur de lis brooch pinned on her candy-pink lapel. She smelled of department store perfume.

Laura asked, "May I come in?"

"I suppose."

Laura smiled, and it wasn't an unkind expression. But as she crossed into the living room, she eyed every spec from the pine beams to the log furniture, from the neatly hung jackets on tree limb pegs to boots for all occasions (snow, mud, hiking, work) lined up beneath. "What an unusual home you have," she said. "It's not at all what I expected."

"What did you expect?"

"Well, I…" Laura looked around. The sun beamed through the picture window, framing the forest garden as if an impossible painting hung on the wall. Herbs pinned to a wire scented the air with thyme, oregano, and sage. Embroidered pillows displayed on Rudy's log sofa brightened the warm wood room with whimsical bees and hummingbirds. "I don't rightly know," said Laura. "But it's simply charming."

Willamina beamed. Indeed, she and Rudy had made a lovely home together. His vision and building along with her organizing and tending to the practicalities of life had come together to create something bigger than them both. "Thank you. Can I get you some tea?"

"That'd be nice." Laura sat the urn on the coffee table next to a display of cracked geodes, a potted rosemary plant, and beeswax candles.

Willamina made and served the tea while Laura poked around, commenting on the neat and tidy pantry, the pristine condition of her cabinets, and did she always keep the place so clean?

When the two women were settled on the couch, Summer Roses teacups in hand, Willamina asked, "So what's this all about?"

"I'm sorry for your loss. But to be honest, we've been a little worried about your husband's passing and you out here on the homestead all by yourself. So, I wanted to offer you some options."

"Options?"

"It must be tough living out here all alone. There's so much upkeep. It will be difficult to do everything by yourself. You're stocked up for the moment, but can you harvest the garden now that your husband is gone? Social security isn't much to survive on. Wouldn't some support be nice?"

Light filtered through the window. Willamina had seen the harsh sun in Arizona, the foggy New Hampshire haze, the sticky Florida rays, and everything between when she and Rudy backpacked across the United States before settling down. But Washington's light was unlike any place else—a pastel softness that lingered well into twilight, sky dotted with pink and lavender clouds, like something supernatural. It reminded her of Rudy.

"What I'm getting at," said Laura, "is we have a lovely retirement home in town, Haven Senior Living. There are shuffleboard tournaments and karaoke competitions. All meals are provided with no cooking on your part. Excellent housekeepers. You wouldn't have to lift a finger, and you'd be surrounded by others of your age. Not alone out here where anything could happen. Doesn't that sound nice?"

"I—"

"Oh, don't worry, it's covered by Medicaid if you qualify, and from what I understand, you've no assets other than this home, and, if that's correct, I can help you liquidate and still retain your benefits. The rooms are furnished. You wouldn't have to move anything. You could forget about cooking, cleaning, harvesting, keeping up the property, and paying bills. Forget everything and enjoy your final chapter with ease."

"Forget?" asked Mrs. Wildemore.

"There wouldn't be anything to worry over. You'd make new friends and—"

"Forget?" asked Willamina again. Forget Rudy's lovingly crafted home, his food forest they'd built with over half a century of their lives? Forget that she'd stood by him, believed in him, and helped make his vision come true? Give up on that? On the animals? On the forest? On nature itself? "What about Rudy?" Willamina asked but to herself, not Laura.

"Oh, there is a perfect spot for his urn. There's a wonderful glass display case in each room. It even has a lock on it. Just put all your treasures on the shelves and lock them up safe."

Willamina pictured Rudy in a glass cabinet, on a manufactured shelf, not wild and free, hair riding the wind, sun deepening the brown of his cheeks. She saw herself next to him doing nothing but frittering away time, surrounded by concrete and plastic flowers, and eating packaged meals. "No," said Willamina.

"No?"

"Rudy and I will stay here."

"I know it's hard," said Laura. "Change is always frightening, but if you'll just see reason—"

"Reason," said Willamina, "is the exact opposite of what I want to see." Willamina stood and walked to the door. "Now, if that is all." She placed her hands on her hips, an action that had only grown in power since her younger days.

Laura sat down her teacup, grabbed her purse, and shuffled to the door.

"I will stop by," said Laura. "Pop in for a friendly visit from time to time if you don't mind."

"Folks have a right to do as they see fit," said Willamina, knowing a refusal would be pointless. Besides, though reason was the last thing she wanted right then, she realized there might be a time when she needed help, when she wasn't as able, when she might welcome a helping hand. Reason had not flown out the door. It had just compromised for the time being.

After Laura left, Willamina piled nuts, plump berries, and fragrant herbs on plates and set them outside as an apology to the animals.

Then Mrs. Wildemore did the most curious thing. More curious than mice making tea or asparagus soup. Or hawks gifting flowers. Or animals saluting. She left a bowl of almond milk out. She had

poured it into one of her Summer Roses
serving bowls, sat it on a charger plate,
garnished it with rosemary stems, and
said as she placed the offering on the
ground, "I want to see what you see,
Rudy."

When Willamina walked into her room
to change the bedding and finally sleep in
their bed, she found it already washed
and remade. Her bluebird embroidered
pillows had been fluffed, and the
bedcovers were turned down. Rudy's eco
urn sat on the nightstand next to a lit
beeswax candle, the air scented with
honey. Without question, she climbed
between the embroidered sheets and said,
"Goodnight," to whoever might be
listening.

In the morning, Willamina checked on the
bowl and plates and found them empty
and, more peculiarly, discovered a book of
some sort placed beside them. A whisper
of a breeze caressed her hair which was
no longer tethered at her neck but white
waves cascading around her middle. Bird
calls filled the trees. Croaks and chatters
and the buzz of bumblebees reminded her

how alive their forest garden was—and indeed, it was *theirs*. Even though Rudy had gone, it belonged in *their* charge. She realized it might have started as Rudy's dream, but in all those years together, her by his side, believing in him, seeing what he brought to life, it had become hers, too. Something she didn't want to live without. It was *their* life. *Their* passion. *Their* vision.

She picked up the tome, a scrapbook with a 1970s floral cover. She fingered it and opened the first page.

A picture of a younger Rudy stared back at her from not ten years after moving into their Trout River homestead. A red squirrel with a bandaged leg curled around his neck, kissing his bearded cheek. Rudy wore that cockamamie grin, and tears leaked from Willamina's eyes.

"Rudy," she said. "My uncontainable Rudy." She held the book to her heart and hugged it. "I thought I'd lost this book decades ago."

A *chuck chuck chuck* sounded next to her. The red squirrel scrambled over and held up his forepaw, showing her the bandage was still in place.

"I see," she said, and the little thing *chuck chucked* again, climbing up on her arm, and pointed at the picture.

"Is that…?" Willamina asked, "Is that your relative?"

The red squirrel bounced up and down, rusty hairs tickling her skin.

"Your mother?"

It shook its head.

"Father?   Grandfather?   Great-grandfather? Great, great, great—?"

The fuzzball nodded and hopped and *chucked*, and Willamina remembered. She remembered with a vividness like a Dolby Cinema film playing on the big screen. Or fireworks lighting up the Fourth of July. Or like Rudy, wild Rudy, standing directly in front of her.

After a hailstorm, Rudy had found the injured red squirrel concussed with a broken arm from golf ball-sized hail. He'd named him Barnaby and nursed him back to health, but the little guy wouldn't leave.

"Red   squirrels   are   notoriously singular," Rudy had said, "but this little one   doesn't   want   to   leave." Indeed, Barnaby   preferred   nestling   in   Rudy's wonderland beard, cracking nuts from the top of Rudy's haloed curls, or using his wire-rimmed glasses to propel himself off

Rudy's head to the couch or kitchen table or wherever else he'd want to go. Barnaby slept nestled between Willamina and Rudy for an entire year before he finally found a gal of his own. Consequently, Barnaby had sired a generation of red squirrels that lived right there on the homestead.

"Well, then, I'll call you BJ for Barnaby Junior," said Willamina, and the squirrel *chucked* his agreement.

Willamina and BJ leafed through the scrapbook, recalling memory after memory as the forest animals returned and circled her: a polaroid of Rudy, overalls equipped with hoe and spade, clutching a bouquet of chamomile, Rudy lying in a patch of sunlight by the pepperings of asparagus, Rudy mending a raccoon, Rudy, that first time they'd ever come to the Little Trout River plot, standing in a barren wasteland, in a downpour, grinning, holding a bright yellow, long-beard hawkweed in his hand.

How had she missed it?

The chamomile tea, the asparagus soup, the raccoon, and hawkweed.

They had been trying to help her remember him the entire time!

A *chirp, chirp, chirp, twitter, trill... chirp, chirp, chirp, twitter, trill* filled the air, the same anthem the birds had sung the day Rudy died. The first time Willamina had heard it, she thought the birds had behaved as if nothing had happened. As if Rudy's passing were inconsequential. But now, she wondered, did it mean something more? Something different?

BJ chattered, hopped, and wagged his rusty-red tail. He tugged on Willamina's ankle-length skirt.

"Okay, okay. I'm coming." She laughed and clutched the scrapbook as the little wire tail pulled her into the forest garden with a procession of animals following.

"What are you trying to show me, now?"

As they passed beneath the grapevine arbor and headed down the path to the walnut tree, Willamina spotted what all the excitement was about.

Rudy's urn, along with their wedding photo, sat at the base of the grandfather tree. Godrays shone down through leafy branches like streamers from a church window. Limbs and bushes, flowers and grasses all moved, swaying together. Around them, piles of fresh berries, plump peaches, honeysuckle flowers, walnuts, and every imaginable bounty from their forest garden were gathered and displayed. Birds fluttered to perches. The harvest mice held almonds in their forepaws, and whitetail, raccoon, rabbits, lizards, and snakes emerged from the forest surrounding Rudy's grand memorial.

A collective voice sounded on the breeze, "We remember Rudy," and then Mrs. Wildemore saw what Rudy had seen.

It started as coagulated mist, sunspots, orbs, and little flashes of lights appearing throughout the forest. On the path. On a branch. A chamomile stem. A leaf.

Willamina blinked. She rubbed her old eyes. A glimmering whole came into view like an intricate, living web weaving throughout the forest and animals. It sparkled and danced, touching everyone and everything as if it breathed in unison with all life. It wrapped its shiny strings around her, and she felt it like a long-missed hug. Everything moved in concert, like an orchestra where different instruments played different parts, making the whole piece rich, complete, and harmonic, and she, she was a part of it.

"We'll always remember Rudy," the collective voice crooned, a lullaby on the wind.

The tears Willamina shed were those of joy. Of relief. Of gratitude so overwhelming, she couldn't form words.

The celebration that followed venerated Rudy more than Willamina could have wished for. They buried his ashes at the walnut tree's roots to nourish the ground. Nasturtium and chamomile petals dropped on top of them, blown by the wind, birds and bees played their music in concert with the breeze, BJ snuggled around Willamina's neck, and everyone indulged in the wild bounty Rudy's vision and hard work had made possible.

In the years to come, Mrs. Ruddle Wildemore would continue her late husband's life's work. *Their* shared life's work. And when Laura visited, Willamina would make sure to amend her will with the cooperation of Fish and Wildlife and designate this place, their home, as a wildlife sanctuary when she died.

Eleven years later, on the very day that Rudy had passed, Willamina headed out to the walnut tree to nap. Huckleberries were fat on the bush, and nasturtiums bloomed like bolts of colored lights on the forest floor. Willamina, at ninety-one, was quite tired. She eased her old bones onto the moss-covered roots. Birds flew down and landed on her lap. The daughter of Barnaby Junior nestled in her arms as Mrs. Ruddle Wildemore closed her eyes for the very last time.

Her body was never found. Some say the earth swallowed her up. Or that bears or wolves carried her away. But the truth of the matter was that nature wrapped Mrs. Willamina Wildemore within its web while birds, reptiles, amphibians, and animals gathered. They made a crown of chamomile and placed it on Willamina's white-haired head while birds sang *chirp, chirp, chirp, twitter, trill*. They covered her body with earth and leaves as Willamina's spirit crossed to join Rudy's, free and uncontained.

And, once every year during summer, if one is open, if one looks, they'll see them gathered there—all the creatures and nature sharing the fruits of the forest garden in memory of the two who dedicated the better parts of their lives to restoring the wild ones' forest home.

See Mande Matthews's story "For the Love of Wild Things" online at Metaphorosis.
If you liked it, leave a comment. Authors love that!
Remember to subscribe to our e-mail updates so you'll know when new stories are posted.

About the story

The first inkling:

I have long been fascinated with permaculture and food forestry, though, I fear, my thumb is blacker than night. I read once that fairies will help you in your garden, though none have bestowed their blessings on mine. Perhaps they see me as the plant murderess that I am. I'm not giving up, though, and still brave the dry Arizona heat in hopes of one day growing my own food.

The second inkling:

During a Method Writing class, I conjured up a memory. (Method Writing, for those who don't know, was invented by Jack Grapes and is based on Method Acting. It teaches writers how to find their deep voice and often involves writing from your own truths to access authenticity.) The memory that brewed to a boil during a Method Writing session was of my father in the funeral home's austere viewing room under flickering fluorescent lights.

My father passed quietly without pomp or circumstance. No memorial. No mourners lined up to pay respects. Though the entire family would later spread his ashes off Dead Horse Point, only my brother, mother, and I were standing there next to him as he lay on that metal hospital-grade gurney. It was as he wanted it. He was a humble man. Yet, he lived a life of service and good work that benefited hundreds if not thousands.

The two inklings became one:

Food forestry and my father's passing (and processing the grief of his loss) magically merged. I don't know how or why; that's left to the creative subconscious. But they did, and the story was born. For the Love of Wild Things is my tribute to my father and all others who have toiled long and hard, made a difference, yet passed from this big beautiful dance of life without much recognition. I can attest that good work, whether seen or unseen, lives on.

A question for the author

Q: What's your favorite type of pie?

A: I believe all pies are created with equal favorability. That said, I try to stick to a low fat, whole food plant-based, low glycemic diet and have yet to find the perfect pie recipe that fits those criteria. If anyone knows of one, I'd be forever grateful if you'd share it.

About the author

Mande Matthews is a fantasy author and award-winning artist. When Mande is not creating or hunting for fairy rings, she helps her husband with his Native

American reservation dog rescue. She lives in the White Mountains of Arizona with her husband and a menagerie of rescued furred, feathered, and special needs animal companions.

MandeMatthews.com, @MandeMatthews

Her Last Will

Karl El-Koura

In the night, the silent robots took away his wife and left a note in her place.

Sensing from his heart rate that he was awake, Toqs' arm band began vibrating with a series of pulses, one for each person wishing to send their condolences. He slapped the band's face to mute the thread without looking at any of the messages.

The note had been printed on a long tent card, placed where his wife had been sleeping. Underneath an access code was the message the robots had printed for him:

HELLO, TOQUER HINGI. WE REGRET TO INFORM YOU THAT **SERENE HINGI**, AGED ONE-HUNDRED-TWENTY-ONE, IS NO LONGER ALIVE. WE INVITE YOU TO WATCH A FIVE-MINUTE CREMATION CEREMONY TODAY AT **09:25** TO COMMEMORATE YOUR WIFE. IF REQUIRED, THE SERVICES OF A GRIEF COUNSELOR ARE AVAILABLE AT NO COST TO YOU FOR THE NEXT TWENTY-FOUR HOURS. HAVE A NICE DAY.

P.S. THIS CODE HAS BEEN PROVIDED TO SERENE HINGI'S FRIENDS AND ACQUAINTANCES.

"No, no, *no!*" Toqs yelled. He looked around the empty bedroom self-consciously. Serene had been catching him talking to himself with increasing frequency over the last few years. But, of course, no one had overheard—the suite was empty except for him.

They'd purchased it once they'd both retired. A place of their own on the outermost ring of the *Adagio*, the space station in orbit around Earth. Toqs loved it. He could sit on the bench of the bay window in their living room and get spectacular views day or night: the moon, the stars, or—his favorite—the spinning Earth, with its daytime blue and green and white, or its pinprick yellow lights of human nocturnal activity. Between that, his books, and his movies, Toqs didn't need much else—except for Serene, who was 'no longer alive', in the gently euphemistic words of the folded piece of plastic paper.

But Serene had become concerned about his mental state.

"You need buddies," she used to say whenever she came home from a power-walk around the ring with friends or a night out to the holos, and caught him talking to himself, or felt sorry for having left him alone.

"I have you," he had always replied. He didn't mind her leaving him for an afternoon or even a night or two; he didn't mind being alone, as he told her repeatedly ... because he knew she'd always come back.

"I'm not enough," she'd said, again and again.

He'd never understood that; she had been enough, and she knew it. But had she also known that one day she might be gone, and he'd be left alone, without the expectation of her return to hang on to?

Of course she'd known; everyone dies.

The bed felt colder than normal. His hands dropped to where she'd been sleeping, and he smoothed out the sheet.

It was just after seven-thirty in the morning.

He wouldn't be allowed to grieve his wife, however. Instead, he'd have to deal with what he knew would be a bureaucratic nightmare. That was his definition of a bureaucracy: a complex system where mistakes were easily made but corrected only with great difficulty.

Still clutching the problematic tent card, Toqs pushed his feet into his slippers and shuffled slowly to the galley kitchen, his old muscles needing time— more time every day, it seemed—to loosen up.

They'd set up their terminal on a table in a little nook opposite the fridge, so they could watch the news from Earth and the stations orbiting it while they cooked.

He pulled back the chair and sat down, then dialed the ring's attendant service. "Hello, I received this card," he said, waving it at the camera when the animated face instantly appeared on the screen.

"I'm sorry for your loss." The attendant's head was human-shaped but metallic, so nobody was tricked even subconsciously into thinking they were speaking to a real person. "Would you like to make use of the complimentary services of our grief counselor?"

"I would like to correct an error you've made." He forced himself to take a deep breath, like Serene had taught him, then continued, more calmly: "My wife did not want to be burned."

"That is the default."

"She sent different instructions. Space burial. She made a point of telling me. Please correct it."

The smile on the animated gray face changed by a calculated percentage toward regret. "No such instructions were received—"

"She sent them. Anyway, you're receiving them now. She made a point of telling me. Maybe because of the cost." Cremation was complimentary, which meant included in the cost of living on the *Adagio*; placing your body into a titanium coffin and shooting you toward deep space was extra. "I don't care about the cost. Can you please correct it?"

"Unfortunately not. Since your wife is no longer alive to provide authorization, I cannot change her funeral instructions."

Karl El-Koura   Metaphorosis

"You said you didn't get any instructions!"

"Correct. The funeral instructions are the default ones, unless new instructions are received."

He leaned back, staring at the metallic face with its eighty percent beatific, twenty percent regretful smile.

In many ways, Toqs felt, this world had been custom-built for him. Almost all of his interactions were automated or with automata, such as the wheeled robots who delivered their groceries or other shopping from the inner rings. When he'd retired after seventy-five years in home systems repair, Serene said that the mental mechanism that allowed him to endure interaction with other people, under so much strain for a century, had finally broken, and he'd sworn off the whole human project. People judged, robots didn't. Neither did animals, like the German Shepherd who'd passed before Toqs had met Serene (a dog he could never bring himself to replace). Robots and dogs were safe, because they didn't make him feel, as clients or acquaintances or even 'friends' did much of the time, as if their eyes were microscopes and he a specimen coming up short.

Occasionally, though, dealing with the rigidity of software could elicit a sense of frustration beyond anything in the power of even the most obtuse person.

Toqs took another deep breath to calm himself; unlike human beings, bots weren't affected by the loss of one's temper. Working himself up with anger would raise his already high blood pressure, and waste his time, and do nothing at all to the equanimous attendant, who was likely having several or maybe even hundreds of simultaneous conversations.

It was quarter to eight.

Toqs began to feel a knot in his stomach and a familiar constriction in his throat, as if his subconscious knew what he'd decided before *he* did. Because he knew enough about the way the software worked to understand that he didn't have time to sort this out with a computer program.

With forced calmness he said, "Can you put me in touch with a human supervisor responsible for burials in this ring?"

He got up and shuffled to the fridge, ordering a glass of cold water for his suddenly very dry mouth.

The animated face blinked a few times, then informed him he was being transferred, and now a harried human face appeared on the screen, a man with drooping eyes and a grizzle of patchwork gray-black stubble along his neck and cheeks.

Always harried, always forcing Toqs to rush through what he needed to say. Which, inevitably, meant nothing came out quite right, and he ended up sounding like an idiot.

"Yes?" the man said without looking at him. The name at the bottom of the screen said ALBUR DRIGIT.

Toqs suddenly didn't know what to do with the glass of water. He took another sip, then set it on the counter.

"Are you there?" Albur Drigit said. "Can you hear me?"

"Hi, yes. I can hear you." He returned to his chair. "The thing is—my wife. She died this morning. Last night, I should say. They took her away. The card said she's to be cremated, okay? But she didn't want that. She wanted—"

"I'm sorry for your loss." He spoke perfunctorily, but Albur's tired eyes flicked over to Toqs to emphasize his sympathy, then flicked away again to one of his other screens. "Name and ID?"

"Toquer Hingi, one-four-nine-eight-oh."

Type, type, type, eyes flick back, half-shut with annoyance and long-suffering. "Not yours, sir—your wife's."

"Oh, sorry," Toqs said, then swallowed again, half-smiled.

Albur stared at him, waiting.

Toqs gave Serene's full name and number.

Type, type, type—pause, scanning, reading. But reading what? Then Albur turned completely away from his other screen and faced Toqs.

For a moment, the professional veneer seemed to have fallen away from Albur's face. He stared at Toqs—but not impatiently like before. His cheeks drooped, as if sadness were weighing down his face. The borrowed confidence from carrying out his duty, the mask of a stressed and harried official, had hidden that sadness.

The moment passed as Albur tried to lift his face with a twitch of a smile. "I see the problem, Mr. Hingi." He spoke hesitantly. "Your—uhm, your wife did provide new funeral instructions about seven months ago—"

"Yes, correct! Around then. Yes!" Toqs was too excited to contain himself. Would it be this easy?

"She didn't complete the form, though. The instructions are still in draft."

"So? It confirms her intentions."

Albur's lips turned up in a skeptical look that seemed much more natural to them than the attempt at a smile. "Maybe her intentions were to think about it more."

"No, no, no." It wasn't going to be easy at all, was it? "She was very clear with me."

"Strictly speaking," Albur said, now fully returned to his efficient bureaucrat persona, "I'm not even supposed to tell you as much as I did."

"I'm trying to make sure she has the burial she wanted. Please."

"Maybe I can help, if you'll speak to a grief counselor. You'd get priority—I could have someone at your place in half an hour."

"What—why?"

Albur rubbed his stubbled chin with his palm. "Grief does strange things to people. It makes them focus on minor things. Emphasize something that wasn't that important to the deceased." He took a long breath and let it out slowly. "I can override her instructions. Submit the form on her behalf. Change everything around. But before doing that, I want to make sure those were really her wishes. Not just your grief talking."

"Yes—I understand. I'll talk to them. But you said at my place. Why does it need to be in person?"

"That's the way they do it now." Albur shrugged. "Maybe they realized they can't hand you a tissue through a screen."

"I don't need to talk to anyone," Toqs said, a little desperately, like a trapped rabbit that knows it's not getting free. But he tried anyway: "I'm fine. I haven't even grieved yet—you people haven't let me. Right now I just want to make sure my wife's wishes are honored."

Albur took another long-suffering breath, then said, "I'm trying to help you, sir. It's your choice. Give me a call back if you change your mind."

"All right. But they can call me here. I won't need tissues."

Toqs spent the next twenty-five minutes pacing his kitchen, his glance bouncing onto and away from the screen, anticipating the call.

The grief counselor didn't ring his terminal, however; she knocked on his door.

"Seriously?" he said out loud.

"We prefer in-person meetings," a woman's voice replied through the door. "I'm Doctor Glazer," she added helpfully.

For a long few moments, he stood rooted to the floor. What kind of grief counselor ignored your wishes and increased your anxiety and already high blood pressure? Weren't they supposed to help calm you?

"Everything okay?" she asked.

He already felt exhausted from his conversation with the unhelpful Albur Drigit. He would've liked to go back to bed for a rest, but the efficient system that processed the deceased as soon as possible—because no one liked to face death these days, or because someone somewhere had determined a quick funeral accelerated the grieving process—wouldn't wait for him.

"Hello?" Dr. Glazer said, a note of concern entering her voice.

In his mind, he could hear Serene say, in that reproachful but kind, understanding, even loving tone: "You're not going to let that poor woman stand out there, are you?"

No, he wouldn't. And not because it was arguably less awkward to let the doctor in than to wait for her to go away. He wouldn't let that poor woman stand out there because he couldn't let Serene down—in this last service he could offer her—due to a temporary social discomfort.

He walked to the front of their home and opened the door. A woman half to a third his age (but, at this stage in his life, almost everyone he encountered was that much younger than him), Dr. Glazer's hair was pulled back in a tight ponytail, and the gentle wrinkles around her lips and green eyes indicated a face, unlike Albur Drigit's, accustomed to smiling.

The echo of Serene's voice played in his mind: "Maybe invite her in?"

He moved out of the way. "Can I get you a drink or something?" When Serene hosted house parties, he had appointed himself on drinks duty—it gave him a chance to escape to the kitchen and recharge every time a new person arrived or when a guest finished their drink. Her friends used to comment to Serene about how helpful and considerate Toqs was, swooping in as soon as he spied an empty glass. She always agreed with them.

"Coffee would be very kind." Dr. Glazer stood in the foyer. She looked around, then back at him, gently smiling.

"I just want my wife buried properly," Toqs said.

"Let's talk about it. Over here?" She indicated the couch in their living room.

"We can go in the kitchen," he said.

"Wherever you're most comfortable."

He turned around to close the door. When she had been especially frustrated with his excuses to get out of socializing, Serene used to call him the human equivalent of a 'wannabe neutrino', trying to minimize his social interactions. She'd made it her project to 'help' him, after he'd retired and his need or desire for isolation had become more prominent. The more he'd resisted, the harder she'd pushed. She'd gone as far as tricking him into social situations, like when she'd convinced him to go to a fancy restaurant with her to celebrate his one-hundred-and-twentieth birthday (he'd long claimed birthday parties were for children only). Of course, once they'd arrived, he'd realized she'd invited everyone they'd ever met on the *Adagio*. ("I never said it would be just the two of us," she'd whispered, smiling innocently, when he shot her a disapproving look at the doors to the restaurant.)

It had been hard to get mad at her; she'd done those things because she loved him. And she'd made him her mission because he'd refused her suggestion of seeking professional help—because he didn't feel there was a problem for a professional to solve. Toqs had been lucky enough to be less neutrino-like when he'd met Serene, and Serene had provided all the social interaction he needed, even setting aside the times she'd forced him to go out and socialize, to have people over to their home, to engage in human interaction. And he did have friends, real friends, although it was true that most of them had by now died and been carried off, burned or buried.

"Mr. Hingi?" Dr. Glazer called.

He closed the door and went to the kitchen.

Dr. Glazer had set herself up at their table, having placed a small tablet in the middle beside their terminal. She asked for permission to transcribe their conversation.

He nodded, then instructed the refrigerator to brew two coffees.

"Tell me about her."

So, slowly and hesitantly at first, he did. Over coffee with a stranger, sitting at the kitchen table where every morning for the last quarter-century he and his wife had had breakfast together, and lunch most days, if she wasn't out, and almost always dinner.

Dr. Glazer was a good listener. Too good. She had a way of nodding and saying "hmm, mhmm" and a warm, Rogerian smile that elicited more words, more stories, more self-revelation.

When he stopped for a moment and realized everything he'd said about the woman he loved and the life they'd shared, he felt stripped naked in front of this stranger. More than naked. He'd once told Serene that he'd only go see a therapist who revealed something about themselves for everything you revealed about yourself. She'd said, "That's not a therapist, Toqs. That's called a friend."

He sat up straighter. "Is that enough, Doctor? Do you have what you need? I'm not beside myself with grief—I'm beside myself with frustration. My wife gave very specific instructions for her burial, but made a mistake and forgot to submit a form. And I just need you to call this guy in charge—this Albur Drigit—and allow me to honor her wishes before it's too late."

He checked his band. 08:58.

After a few moments of staring at him, Dr. Glazer leaned back in the chair and crossed her legs. "I'll send the message," she said. "I'll do it right now, while we finish up. I would like you to answer one last question, Mr. Hingi. What will you do now that your wife has passed?"

He opened his mouth to give a glib response, but closed it again quickly; in that moment, he realized he didn't trust himself to answer. He felt that saying *anything* would cause him to burst into tears in front of this stranger. Because he knew exactly what the rest of his life would be like: here, in this apartment, his world consisting of the four rooms of the suite, spending morning to night sitting on the bench by the window, endlessly watching or waiting for the spinning day-night of the planet where he'd made so many memories with Serene.

"I don't know," he said finally. "Right now I'm focused on burying my wife."

Dr. Glazer nodded, closed her tablet. She stood.

Toqs cleared the empty cups from the table, breathing more freely. That was it; it was done. Serene would be launched into deep space, like she wanted.

He walked Dr. Glazer to the door. She told him about a support group she ran for people who'd lost their spouse, but he nodded without taking in any of the details. As soon as she was gone, he returned to the bedroom and sat on the bed gently, then let himself fall back onto the mattress. He could've slept for hours, but Serene's ceremony was in fifteen minutes.

He pushed his exhausted body out of the bed and into the kitchen. He hesitated at the refrigerator—he was tempted to order a long island iced tea, Serene's favorite drink. But alcohol, especially on an empty stomach, messed up his digestion. He settled on a second cup of coffee instead.

Toqs looked at the tent card's code and wished Dr. Glazer had offered to stay, so he wouldn't have to watch by himself as his wife was buried.

Grabbing the cup of brewed coffee, he lowered himself into the chair and showed the tent card to the screen. The view changed to a black background with white lettering:

FUNERAL CEREMONY OF SERENE HINGI

(CREMATION)

COMMENCING IN—

—with a timer counting down from thirteen minutes.

Toqs stabbed his finger into the attendant call button. "It's not supposed to be a cremation," he said to the animated face. But there was no time to waste. "Put me in touch with Albur Drigit, please."

The animated eyes rolled in their sockets for a few moments, then their gaze resettled on Toqs. "Albur Drigit's terminal is not responding," the bot said. "Would you like me to try again in five minutes and notify you?" There was a shift in the bot's voice, as if reading a new set of instructions. "Alternatively, Albur Drigit is available for in-person meetings while his terminal is malfunctioning."

"Where is he?"

The address was on the other side of the ring ... *thirty* minutes away if Toqs ran at his top speed from fifty or sixty years ago. He had only one viable option: the supersonic carriages that spun around the ring. Normally he would've done anything to avoid being trapped in a small sphere with a dozen or more strangers. Today was abnormal, however. He was already out of his apartment and shuffling toward the stop, where a carriage was boarding. He only just made it inside as it spun up and took off, full with morning commuters.

Toqs hardly noticed the ride, he was so focused on getting to Albur Drigit and fixing the instructions before it was too late. If it wasn't already. At one point, though, he became aware that a small child, maybe six or seven, was staring at him from across the carriage. Toqs stuck out his tongue and she giggled; then she returned the favor, sticking out her little tongue and making him smile. Like robots and German Shepherds, children were all right.

A few stops later, Toqs unclipped himself and stepped off, eyes scanning the directions on the walls. He walked quickly, pushing his aching legs, unused to this kind of activity, until he reached Albur Drigit's door. One more minute until the ceremony. Too late?

Albur answered his furious knocking.

"You've made a huge—" Toqs began breathlessly.

"It's all right," Albur said, then hesitantly reached out a hand and placed it on Toqs' shoulder. Even hunched over, he towered over Toqs. "Come in."

Inside, a projection wall faced a couch, a small plastic table between them. Toqs stared at the couch; one side, which Albur clearly preferred, had a deep impression. The original black of the fabric, evident in the rest of the couch, had turned almost gray in that favored spot.

Albur asked him to sit down, then instructed the screen to turn on.

On the wall, a view of Serene appeared. She lay in a titanium casket, her head resting on a white pillow, while a soft sound—the chanting of many people in low voices—seemed to reach out and envelop her and Toqs in their separate rooms.

He glanced over at Albur, upset that circumstances had led him to experience such an intimate event in the presence of a stranger. Immediately he remembered that, less than thirty minutes earlier, he'd wished he wouldn't have to be alone as his wife was buried—so which one was it?

Albur's eyes were fixed on the screen.

Toqs turned his attention back to the ceremony. The soft sound of the harmonious chanters filled his heart with a strange mixture of hope and sadness. He stared at his wife's resting face—her closed eyes—as if this were a morning like any other and he could lean over and wake her with a kiss.

When the chant was finished, a metallic hand closed the top of the casket and sealed it; her name, number, birth date and today's date were marked in gold lettering on the silver lid. The robot picked up the casket as if it weighed nothing and walked it across the white-walled circular room to an open port in the wall. The port accepted the casket, then accelerated it down the airlock tube, faster and faster, and fired it out the external side. The view followed as the casket sailed through the blackness of space, then the same information—her name and number and dates—appeared at the bottom of the screen as the titanium coffin receded from view.

Toqs swallowed hard. Turning to look at Albur, he said, "Thank you for arranging that. But why didn't you update the description? I wouldn't have come barging over here."

"You're not bothering me," Albur said, rubbing the stubble on his cheek nervously as he met Toqs' gaze. "Would you like something to drink? I've taken the rest of the day off."

"It's nine-thirty in the morning."

"I thought maybe you could use a drink." And suddenly, in the other's sad, lonely eyes, Toqs saw that this man half his age wanted him to stay. For his own or for Albur's benefit, Toqs didn't know.

With effort he pushed himself to his throbbing legs. A drink didn't sound so bad, actually; keeping off his feet for a little longer sounded even better. But best to go home. The last thing he needed, on this day more than any other, was to involve himself with another person's problems.

Albur kept sitting. "I think your wife didn't submit the form on purpose."

The tall man's tone was quiet, conspiratorial. Was he accusing Serene of something? "What?" Toqs snapped.

"She left a note in the form." Albur spoke calmly. "There's prompts, you know —any other instructions, any concerns, words you want said at the ceremony. But she wrote, 'My only concern is that my husband will bury himself instead of me when I die. If you can find a way to get him out of our apartment, on this day at least, I'd sure appreciate it and think kindly of you.'"

Toqs was shaking his head. How could she? Saying that—about *him*—to *strangers*!

"That upsets you?" Albur said, watching him as if studying a fascinating specimen.

"You didn't know her," Toqs said defensively.

"I wish I had," Albur said, rising to his feet. "Let me get you a drink and you can tell me about her."

"She wanted to *fix* me. She couldn't just leave it alone."

"Leave what alone? You?"

"Not me." Toqs shook his head in impatience, frustrated by his inability to convey to this stranger the complex relationship he and Serene had shared. "I just want to be left alone!" he blurted out.

The man towering over him said in a quiet voice, "Maybe she understood you enough to know that you don't want that? Not really."

"Don't speak to me like you know me."

Albur's face remained calm, still.

"And you went along with her plan?" Toqs went on, speaking more coldly. All morning he'd been holding at bay a deep anger toward his wife. Not because she'd forced him out into the world—she'd been doing that ever since they'd met—but for leaving him once and for all. And now, being able to redirect it at Albur allowed him to set that anger loose. "You manipulated me, too? You lied to me? How do you think your supervisors are going to feel about that?"

A dark cloud had formed on Albur's broad face. But when he spoke, his voice was still calm and soft. "How do you think people feel about the guy responsible for burying their loved ones? How do *you* feel about me? You want me to do my job, then you want to forget about me as quickly as possible, right? Hold up your band. I'll send you my supervisor's identification number so you can report me."

Toqs didn't move.

"Your wife seems like a very sweet person," Albur said, dropping his arm. "I was happy to do something nice for her." He continued to stare down at Toqs. "You can take what she did in a bad way if you want. Probably being angry is easier than being sad. But I'll tell you this: I wish I had someone in my life who cares about me the way your wife cared about you."

Toqs returned the stare but refused to speak. He wouldn't validate anything this stranger, who knew nothing about Serene or the relationship they'd shared for almost ninety years, had to say about her. After a few moments of silence, he turned and left the sad, lonely man in his sad, lonely apartment.

It would be a long walk back. Briefly he considered taking the carriage. It hadn't been too bad earlier, and the little girl had put a smile on his face. But maybe not today.

He leaned against the wall to gather his strength, then remembered that he'd muted the thread related to Serene. He brought up his arm and glanced through the many messages that had come in that morning, as well as newer ones that continued to pop up, telling him how beautiful her ceremony had been. Serene was gone—and her body receding further away by the minute—but even the quick glance through the things her friends had written made her feel present again.

He allowed his arm to drop. He would read the messages more carefully later.

He'd also have to write everyone back. Some people he hadn't spoken to in a long, long while. He wondered how they were doing.

Slowly he made his way down the hallway, toward his own part of the ring. Albur Drigit *was* a sad man, wasn't he? What kind of person took the day off of work to … what? Listen to an old man's stories about his deceased wife?

And Albur really had no idea, did he? Serene had been a complex person, with good and great and bad and terrible qualities and quirks, with her own issues that Toqs had tried to help her work through. And maybe Serene had been able to see past Toqs' fears and worries; maybe she had understood that he needed a push out into the world. But on this day? As her last act? *Selfless*, Albur would probably say; but Toqs could equally say: stubborn and determined to accomplish her mission. Toqs knew his wife and Albur didn't.

He stopped walking. His breathing had become shallower as he'd worked himself up with these thoughts. He wanted to march back to Albur's door and tell him all of it, explain why it wasn't as simple as Albur had it figured in his head.

But it wasn't worth the effort. Albur wouldn't understand. He couldn't.

Toqs pushed his feet forward.

Maybe Dr. Glazer's group of widows and widowers could understand. If only Toqs had bothered to listen to any of the details.

Someone like Albur could never understand. Even if the sad, lonely man had seen something in Serene's last wish that had inspired him to play along. And if he thought *that* had been selfless, Albur should hear about all the other things Serene had done for Toqs and many others throughout her life.

Albur wouldn't hear those stories, though. Because Toqs wanted to go home to his own apartment. An empty apartment that wasn't going anywhere.

In his mind, he heard Serene's voice again: "You're not going to let that poor man think you're mad at him, are you? Or, even worse"—her voice rose an octave when she pretended to be offended—"that you're mad at *me*!"

He stopped, let out a long sigh.

No, he wouldn't let that poor man think those things—especially not that Toqs was anything but still madly in love with his wife. Not because of a temporary social discomfort.

He turned around, shuffled back to Albur's door.

When the tall man answered, Toqs said, "I'll have that drink now. Long island iced tea." Before Albur could respond, Toqs added quickly, "If the offer still stands—I can tell you about that wonderful woman you just buried."

The heavy, stubbled cheeks lifted. "I'd like that very much," Albur said, stepping out of the doorway to let Toqs in.

See Karl El-Koura's story "Her Last Will" online at Metaphorosis.
If you liked it, leave a comment. Authors love that!
Remember to subscribe to our e-mail updates so you'll know when new stories are posted.

About the story

Hello, my name is Karl El-Koura, and I'm an introvert.

Do they have support groups for introverts, or does no one show up?

I suspect most writers are on the introversion end of the spectrum. Who else would voluntarily lock themselves up alone in a room for hours on end?

Many of my stories, like "Her Last Will", turn out to be about people needing to step outside their comfort zones to connect with other human beings.

This isn't a conscious decision most of the time, but emerges as I think about or write the story and get to know the characters. Perhaps, in the absence of a support group, I use writing to push back against my introverted tendencies.

A question for the author

Q: What is your favorite word?

A: The word that immediately comes to mind is "onomatopoeia". Boom! (When I first learned the word in high school, I thought it was the neatest thing —the way it looked, the way it sounded, even that there was a word to describe words that sound like themselves. Its only drawback is I always have to look up how to spell it.)

About the author

Karl El-Koura lives with his family in Canada's capital city, holds a second-degree black belt in Okinawan Goju Ryu karate, and works a regular job in daylight while writing fiction at night. "Her Last Will" is his second appearance in *Metaphorosis*. His fantasy short story "The Azurian Shield" was published in October 2021.

Portals and Other Lost Things

Elizabeth Rankin

There was no indication that the holes Sylvie accidentally knitted into her first scarf would be portals in space and time.

Her grief counselor had practically insisted she find something to do, now that she'd had three years to grieve over Doug, even if she didn't leave the house to do it. The counselor had meant watercolors or soap making — not breaking the laws of physics.

Outside of a little gardening and cooking for Doug, Sylvie had never pursued a form of artistic expression. The day-to-day was enough. Working, taking care of the girls' homework or practices, and the yearly vacations with Doug at the wheel of the minivan. Sylvie's heart clenched. She didn't cry every time she thought about the past, and that was progress.

A twelfth hole appeared while she wasn't paying close attention to the pattern and Sylvie sighed. Out of habit she looked around for support, someone to laugh with, and saw the smiling faces on the mantle. Framed photos of goofy grins from summer vacations to House on the Rock and Mystery Hole, fully immersed in the kitsch. At the end of the row was an empty frame from the last trip she and Doug had taken, to the Corn Palace. She'd never gotten the photo printed out, never gotten around to checking it off their travel bucket list.

Sylvie got up to take the yawning black hole of the frame away. It reminded her of the last time things had been normal. Of Doug. Of the fact she hadn't left the city in the three years since the funeral. Learning how to do things on her own was challenge enough. Mowing the grass. Dealing with plumbers. Remembering what TV shows she'd always meant to go back and watch, since Doug wasn't interested. It took a year and a half before

she got through a day without crying.
Planning a trip on her own was far outside
her comfort zone. She'd never done it.
Trips could go a million different ways
she'd never had to think about and wasn't
sure she wanted to start.

Her daughters checked in on her, but
they had their own lives. Emma lived six
hours away. Madelyn had two kids of her
own now. They went camping or on bike
tours, active excursions to keep the kids
entertained. Too much for her, they said,
but they'd invite her when they did a
different type of vacation. Better for her to
stay safe at home.

She returned to the recliner,
determined to ignore the holes in her
lovely variegated blue yarn and finish the
damned scarf. She wasn't sure how the
holes had gotten there and couldn't figure
out a way to fix them. Nothing in the book
she'd bought online talked about it, so it
could be an advanced technique. This last
one was right in the middle, where it
couldn't be ignored. A black gap where
yarn should be, small as the tip of her
ring finger.

Sylvie squinted at the hole. It was too
dark. Had it always been like that? A

matte black with no shine, no hint of light. She jabbed a finger through.

Something cold and wet nuzzled her fingertip. Like a nose. She pulled back with a yelp. Sylvie didn't have a pet. Hadn't for a long time.

She tried again, tentative. Soft fur brushed her skin. Sylvie checked her lap for anything that could be mistaken for an animal. She might have been letting the house go a little, but surely not enough to have animals crawling into the furniture. There was nothing but yarn and her stretchiest sweatpants.

She shook all nine inches of scarf she'd managed to complete so far, pulled it taut, and held it out in front of her. All the holes remained black no matter what she held them against, even when she brought her eye up to stare through. No beige carpet. No oversized picture of the family at Dinosaur World, Kentucky. No light. Sylvie turned the scarf over, pushed her finger through the same hole from the other side, and again fur moved under her finger.

Her phone chirped and she jumped. It kept chirping until she fumbled with the swipe to accept the call.

"Hello?" Her voice cracked and she cleared her throat.

"Mom? Are you ok?"

Maddie, her eldest daughter, lived in town and was the worrier now that Sylvie lived alone. The first year without Doug, Sylvie had broken a bone in her hand and not gotten it looked at. At her age, everything hurt anyway. Doug would have bundled her to the ER. Now that he wasn't here, Maddie-the-nurse felt it was her duty to manage her mother's health. Sylvie just wanted to ignore it.

"Oh, I'm fine," Sylvie said. "Doing some knitting."

She eyed the holes and weighed whether to say anything to her daughter. Would she believe it without seeing it? Sylvie wasn't sure she'd believe it herself, and knowing her daughter, Maddie would schedule a barrage of psychiatric visits and CT scans.

"Ok, you sounded surprised," Maddie said. "We're still on for tea tomorrow at three?"

"Oh." Sylvie stroked the lumps in her scarf and tried desperately to think of an excuse to put off the visit. "I forgot tomorrow was Thursday."

It wasn't that she didn't love her daughter, but the visits with just the two of them were strained with Maddie's worry. She would do all the work, bustling around the kitchen like she owned it, not Sylvie. Saying things like 'you rest' and 'you take it easy'.

"Are you not feeling well again?" Maddie's voice sharpened. "I knew the doctor was being lazy. I can make an appointment for this afternoon. Dr. Runyon has openings."

"No, no," Sylvie said. "I just forgot what day it was. They all blend together."

She winced, knowing it was the wrong thing to say. The silence on the other end of the phone confirmed it. Maddie would be on guard tomorrow, looking for signs of deterioration. Sylvie dropped the scarf. Maybe she'd been too long inside after all.

"For tomorrow," Maddie said, neutral, "I'm whipping up a few types of sandwiches. I found watercress, and I'll have ham, egg, and chicken salad. It'll be a fancy tea, just like that show you like."

"Downton Abbey. I finished watching that a few months ago," Sylvie said, a bit too sharp. She tried again, "I've already made the brownies. And I'll make the deviled eggs tomorrow."

One of her greatest disappointments was that her daughters loved Doug's mother's deviled egg recipe instead of her version. Probably because the secret ingredient Doug's family added was sugar, which Sylvie privately thought was disgusting. She could have bought vinegar and capers to make them her way this time, but she didn't want to disappoint Maddie.

Maddie made small talk, then said her goodbyes. The house fell silent. Its emptiness gaped from the hallways and doors, threatening to swallow Sylvie. In her lap, the scarf was a puddle of warmth. More warmth than was natural. A hole leading to a dog was one thing. What was in the others? Would she poke a finger into an acid volcano or a killer plant?

She set the scarf on the arm of the recliner and went to make herself a drink. A good scotch solved many ills.

Glass in hand, Sylvie lay the scarf on the kitchen table. The unnatural blackness of the holes was still there. Light from the fluorescent bulbs illuminated the fabric like it was on an operating table. Nothing about the uneven lines or broken pattern seemed unusual. There weren't any strange symbols accidentally formed by her novice stitches. The yarn had come from the craft store, not an old fortune-teller or mysterious box found in the attic. All appearances said it was a totally ordinary, badly knitted scarf. Something called a straight stockinette pattern, more or less.

Could she have made something magic, without knowing? Or was it some kind of *Twilight Zone* thing, with forces in the universe at work far beyond her understanding? Sylvie wasn't sure what to do next. Doug would have tested the holes. He probably would have made a game of it, rolling dice to decide which he'd poke next. He'd have made sure it was safe first, then invited her to try it, like when they'd gone on the hot sauce factory tour. No one was here to do that for her now.

She swore and knocked back the rest of the scotch. How many more adventures did she have left?

The atmosphere on the other side of the second hole washed her skin with baking heat. When she wiggled her finger, it touched sand. A strong gust of wind pelted grains against her skin. She pulled the opening to her nose and tried to breathe in, hoping for the brine of ocean water, to help tell her where it was. There was nothing, like no air came through at all. Did the holes lead to places on earth, or somewhere else? Calling them 'holes' seemed wrong. They were doorways. Portals that could go anywhere.

She licked her finger and tried to get sand to stick, imagining tiny spots of amethyst and ruby, but the granules fell in the wind or were pushed off by the yarn before she could pull them through. Even stretching the scarf, the clumsy weave was too tight to get more than a single finger through. Sylvie picked at the knit to widen the opening. Energy flickered, like a dying fluorescent bulb. Flashes of the wood veneer underneath the scarf blinked through the blackness. When she stopped plucking, the dark oval stabilized. Delicate things, these portals, if all it took to destroy them was breaking the weave. Which might be good to know.

Snowflakes melted on her body heat in the third portal, and in the fourth something smooth and lush as rose petals flowed against her finger. Each time, she turned the scarf over to be sure they went to the same place from both sides, and they always seemed to. In the fifth hole she felt nothing. Then a tiny pinch, and more, a swarm of miniscule creatures with teeth testing her flesh. Sylvie yelped and yanked her finger back, slapping her palm over the opening.

Could they get through? She waited. Nothing bit into her hand and when she raised it no murderous gnats escaped.

She'd been lucky so far. There were seven holes left that could hold anything. Sylvie folded the scarf to cover all the openings. This was not her imagination. It was dangerous. And impossible.

Someone should know about it. She picked up her phone and looked up the number for NASA. Or was this a national security issue? If nothing could come through, it couldn't cause a problem. Could it? A scientist would want to study this, that was certain. They'd take it away from her, run a lot of tests, and send her on her way.

It could be worth money, she considered, as she eyed the scarf over another, very small, drink. She could sell tickets. To what, though? It was like one of the old attractions, where you stuck your hand into a box and guessed what was inside. No one did that anymore. Who'd want to pay to have their finger chewed on by bugs?

Energy drained out of her. She should mail it to NASA anonymously. If they didn't find anything they'd just think she was a weird lady who liked to knit scarves for astronauts.

What would Doug do?

Throw it out, probably. Once those gnats started biting, he'd say it wasn't worth the risk. He was very practical and usually right. Like when she'd kept raw chicken too long and they'd gotten food poisoning. This could be worse. If those bugs were toxic, like a rattlesnake, she could have died right there on the kitchen floor.

Sylvie opened the drawer to the trash and stared at the paper towels and wrinkled tea bags. The scarf, for all its failings, she'd made on her own. That was what everyone said she should be doing now. Making her own choices. She'd picked out the yarn and the pattern and learned the method. Then she'd made something amazing, something no one else had ever done. It didn't belong in the garbage. Sylvie tucked the scarf into the refrigerator, on the foil covering the pan of cheesecake brownies. It was the best place she could think of for an unidentified and possibly magic object.

Between the sturdy doors, the cold, and the delicious baked goods, anything that got out of those holes might stop there.

It took her a long time to go to sleep. She stared at the picture on her nightstand. Their honeymoon, at Wigwam Village in Arizona. Doug had taken a shot of her from behind, steps away. His hand got into the frame, wrist and fingers blocking the top of one of the wigwams as he reached for her. She stared at that hand every night, though lately she'd also started staring at the back of her head. Back then, her hair had been long, and streamed in the wind as she stood on the hood of the car. It had probably been their best trip, driving Route 66, stopping at every roadside attraction that caught their eye.

The back of the frame held a list of all the places they'd wanted to go. Some crossed off. Some, like the Bonnie Springs wild west resort, had closed. What was left would be enough to fill her time for the rest of her life, if she ever left the city again.

Her finger rubbed back and forth against her palm, still feeling the hard edges of the portal sand, from a beach she'd never seen.

As soon as she woke up enough to remember, Sylvie hurried to the refrigerator and pulled the door open enough to peer inside. The scarf sat on the tinfoil, undisturbed, as far as she could tell. Sylvie unfolded its length and touched the holes, in that just-roused state where the previous day's memories could have been a dream.

No animal nudged her finger in the first hole, but the others blew snow and sand like she remembered.

This was beyond her. She needed some advice, and Maddie would be a good place to start. Sylvie rolled up the scarf and put it back into the refrigerator. After a piece of toast and a shower, she took out all the materials for the eggs. The scarf sat there, waiting, each time she opened the refrigerator door, until Sylvie had to do something with it.

While the eggs boiled, she got paper and a pencil and started a list of portals, numbering 1-12. Those last seven blanks gaped at her until the timer went off. If there was some way to reduce the risk of exploring, they could do it together without Maddie fretting. Sylvie fished the eggs out of the water with a spoon and put them aside to cool. She stared at the spoon, then set it down with a clatter and ran to get the scarf.

The spoon wouldn't fit in any of the holes, but other things might. The end of a knife. A pencil. Tweezers. She gathered them all and used one at a time to try to pull sand from the hole, which seemed the safest option. If she had proof, Maddie couldn't try to say she was losing her mind. The knife and pencil brought back nothing. The tweezers, though — when Sylvie opened them above her hand, tiny sparkles fell from them and brushed against her skin. She closed her fist and laughed. It was real.

She pulled out sand until there was enough to see. Things could come back through if they were attached to her side, it seemed. Against the white of a paper towel, it glinted not red or purple, but green. A search revealed there were beaches on Earth with green sand, including in Hawaii and the Galapagos Islands and a lake in Norway she couldn't pronounce. Hawaii had the only animatronic teddy bear museum in the US, and a life-size whale statue, which would be fun, although the sand could have just as easily have been from Mars for all she knew.

Her phone buzzed with a message from Maddie: "On my way!"

Sylvie folded the paper towel and slid it under her saucer at the table with the unfinished list and set of tweezers. She'd have to wait for the right time to bring it up, test the waters to see how Maddie would react. Sylvie made the eggs, automatically tipping in sugar and mashing up the yolks. Like she'd done a hundred times, or a thousand. She still didn't like them this way. They needed vinegar, and a pinch of dill. A spoonful of pickle relish would be about right. Maddie might be angry, but Sylvie couldn't resist.

She chuckled when she thought of Doug's face, appalled, but the laugh choked in her throat as it flipped to grief. That's how it went. Things seemed fine, until they weren't.

When Maddie arrived, Sylvie returned her daughter's hug with vigor. It felt almost like Christmas, like a secret she'd kept was about to be revealed. There would be wide eyes, but then if she'd done it right, excited smiles.

"You're in a good mood," Maddie said, holding out a set of plastic boxes, heavy with food. "Are you hungry? I brought way more than we need."

"Starving!" Sylvie took the two containers and set them on the counter with a flourish.

Maddie beamed, but her eyes flicked over Sylvie, who tried to tone down her enthusiasm. She didn't want to get Maddie worked up before she had a chance to tell her what was going on.

Maddie set sandwiches on plates while Sylvie prepared the tea.

"What's in these eggs?" Maddie asked after popping one in her mouth.

"Pickle relish," Sylvie said as she brought over the tea caddy.

"You used a different recipe?"

Sylvie couldn't quite tell if the reproach she expected was present in her daughter's tone.

"Well, the kind you've always had were your father's version, not mine." Sylvie sat, not sure why she was talking about this now. "I never liked them. Not with sugar."

"Really?" Maddie's eyebrows were up practically in her bangs. Then she put another on her plate. "I never knew that. Brandon's family puts butter in theirs."

Sylvie braced for more, for admonitions about betraying Doug's traditions — the family traditions — but Maddie patted her mother's arm.

"You can have the eggs any way you want them," Maddie said.

Sylvie tried a smile, but it came out watery. They loaded plates and chatted about everything the grandkids were doing. In the back of Sylvie's mind was the green sand, the fur, and the unknown. Tweezers wouldn't tell them much about the other side. A camera of some kind would be better. Not a selfie stick, that would be too big. She needed one of those cameras they used in surgeries. Like her yearly colonoscopy.

"Can you get a surgical camera at home?" Sylvie realized after she stared into her daughter's surprised face that she had interrupted whatever they were supposed to be talking about.

"A surgical camera?" Maddie's brows furrowed. Sylvie cleared her throat, trying to act casual.

"You know, like the ones they use in going down your throat and looking into your stomach."

"Laparoscopic cameras? Why would you want one of those?" Maddie frowned and straightened her back, eyes narrowed. "You're not going to look in your own stomach, are you?"

"What? No. Don't be ridiculous. How could you think that?"

"I'm just making sure, Mom. You've been cooped up in here by yourself for a couple years, who knows what stuff you've been listening to."

Sylvie felt a scowl drawing her mouth down and took a sip of tea to rearrange her thoughts.

"It's not that. For cleaning." The lie slipped off Sylvie's tongue. This wasn't the right way to start. "I can't remember the last time I cleared out the vents and want to check what's down there."

"Oh, you can get them online," Maddie said, taking a packet of artificial sweetener. Not a sugar cube, like she used to. "Just promise if you are thinking about any medical procedures, you ask me first, ok?"

She smiled like she was joking, but the vigilance in her eyes remained.

"So, what are you doing this summer?" Sylvie changed the subject to travel, something fun and relaxing, that might make Maddie more receptive. "I know you said you were thinking about going out to the Grand Canyon."

"Yep, we're going in the beginning of June. It's going to be hot, but you've got to go when the kids are off, you know?"

The Grand Canyon was close to the giant Lumberjacks at Northern Arizona University. They'd talked many times about crossing them off the list and seeing the Grand Canyon at once, but Maddie didn't mention the statues or the list. The taste of tea lingered in bitter edges on Sylvie's tongue.

"Mom, you look weird," Maddie said. "What's wrong?"

"It's just — are you going to see the Lumberjacks?"

Maddie paused, took a sip of tea, "Are those on your list?"

Sylvie winced at the 'your'. She counted to ten like she had when the girls were small.

"Number 59," Sylvie said.

"Oh." Maddie made her smile gentle. It wasn't her real smile. Sylvie would know; she was still Maddie's mother, after all. "I don't think we'll make it. The kids want to do more hiking."

Did kids like to hike that young? Maddie's boys were just eleven and nine.

"We took you girls all over the country. We had fun." Sylvie's voice quavered at the last, unexpectedly. She found herself looking into her daughter's eyes, searching them for confirmation. Maddie's face crinkled into genuine smile lines.

"Yes, of course we did. But that was your thing, you and Dad."

She didn't say 'and not ours', but she didn't need to. Sylvie understood. The normal places were enough for Maddie. Seeing it so clearly knocked something loose in her. Sylvie felt curiously balanced, on the edge of grief and determination.

"There are a lot of places to cross off," Sylvie said. "I still want to go."

That's why she'd stuck her fingers in those holes.

"Mom." Maddie put her hand over her mother's. It was slightly sticky from the brownie. "You can't go on those trips by yourself, it's not safe. But that's ok. You can do other things. Make your own list, just for you."

Sylvie looked down and swirled her tea. It made sense and was even what her grief counselor had said. Why she'd taken up knitting in the first place. She blinked and saw herself in the recliner, hunched over her knitting and watching old TV shows until she died. The balanced scales inside her tipped to determination.

"Actually," Sylvie said, "I've already started one. I haven't gotten very far yet."

She tapped the paper under her saucer, the one she was going to show Maddie with the portals listed on it.

"That's great, Mom." She patted her hand and pulled away. "You can try out different deviled egg recipes."

Maddie laughed and Sylvie managed a chuckle. Her daughter didn't ask to see the list, as Sylvie had expected. Instead she rose and excused herself to go to the bathroom.

Sylvie half-heartedly gathered courage to tell her daughter about the portals when she got back. Then Maddie strode in and started cleaning the dishes. Sylvie scrambled to her feet, unprepared.

"That's okay, Mom, you take it easy," Maddie said. Just like Sylvie should have known she would.

The confession stuck in her throat as she brought plates to the sink for her daughter to clean. They finished up over idle chatter and hugged their good-byes.

Maddie suggested that Sylvie knit everyone scarves for Christmas, left half the food behind 'to make sure you've got enough to eat, Mom', and hurried out the door to pick the kids up from after-school activities.

Sylvie let her go. The paper still sat folded on the table. Grief still tugged at her, for what was, and what wouldn't be. Maddie would never let her do anything with the portals, that was clear. She went to the fridge and took the scarf out, unsure of what to do alone. The fabric didn't feel as cold as she thought it should, just bumpy from her uneven progress. She lay the scarf amongst the salad plates and crumpled napkins on the table, as if it belonged there with the rest of her things.

Careful not to spill the sand, she pulled the tweezers free from her folded list and slid them into hole number six. They skidded across a smooth surface before encountering soft resistance. She snapped them open and closed until they grabbed on to something, and then she pulled. What came out was a white paper square, crimped around the edges. A cocktail napkin.

"Bonnie Springs Steak House now open." Sylvie read the words the second time out loud, because they didn't make sense at first.

She turned the napkin over in her hands. The words didn't change. Written in a wild west type popular in the midcentury, the ink crisp and the paper as clean as if they'd been delivered yesterday. Tears clouded her vision.

Bonnie Springs, number 11 on the list she and Doug had made, had closed five years ago. Not on enough people's travel plans, apparently. It certainly wasn't on Maddie's. Her daughter's mantle full of photos would be different, and no amount of waiting for the right time was going to change that.

Sylvie took out her list and wrote out 'Bonnie Springs' as the destination of portal six. Her heart thrummed. It wasn't too late for her to go on her own.

She turned the paper over and took Maddie's advice to make her own list. There was a lot to do. First, she'd get a camera to explore the other portals. Then learn to make her own and see if she could control where they went. The last step would be finding a way to make a hole big enough to climb through. Once she figured out how she'd done the smaller ones, Sylvie could try using some of that giant, novelty yarn they used to make those puffy knit blankets. She chuckled at the idea of squeezing through one of those. Doug would have gone, and so could she.

Sylvie put the final action item of making a portal for herself at the very bottom. There would be more challenges along the way to add in. She might never get through everything, but she had to try. If she'd made holes in the fabric of the universe on accident, Sylvie could only imagine what she could do on purpose.

See Elizabeth Rankin's story "Portals and Other Lost Things" online at Metaphorosis.
If you liked it, leave a comment. Authors love that!
Remember to subscribe to our e-mail updates so you'll know when new stories are posted.

About the story

"Portals and Other Lost Things" started from a writing prompt during "Story a Day May" in 2020, although I can't remember the original prompt. Like so many people, I was feeling stuck inside and longing to visit other places, hoping they'd still be around after the pandemic. I was also trying out new hobbies, although knitting (as featured in my story) wasn't one of them.

The first version was as a flash-length revenge story, where my protagonist decides to make her ex disappear through the portals in her scarf. I felt that version was too safe, and my critique group agreed. What I really wanted to do was to explore what would make someone want to take a leap and go through the unknown.

There's a sense of general expectation that after you hit mid-life, you retire from being interesting. This is particularly true for women in our culture. I just hit that stage in my own life, so I might be a little sensitive about it! I wanted to write something that shows that strange things can happen to anyone, and maybe your later years are your most dynamic.

I rewrote the story as a more thoughtful internal narrative to take the reader from where Sylvie is stuck in the expectations of others to how she shakes loose from them. I also wanted to create a little bit of mystery with the portals so some things remain unknown, like how they work and where they go. My beta readers wanted to know more, and that was the point. There's still plenty of life left to explore, even if you're not sure how you're going to get there.

A question for the author

Q: Do you live near where you were born? Have you traveled much?

A: I actually live right down the road from the hospital where I was born! Not on purpose. I left the area for about 10 years, and didn't intend to come back, but fate (a.k.a. the need for a job) intervened. I enjoy traveling and have been to Europe a few times, as well as Mexico and Canada. One of my life goals is to visit every National Park. I've been to 13 so far, out of 63, so that should keep my vacations full for a very long time. Especially because they keep adding them! I'd like to see more of the world, and more of the U.S. as well. There are more fascinating places to go than I'll ever have time for, but I can try!

About the author

Elizabeth Rankin is the daughter of a librarian and grew up telling stories in the stacks. She worked in publishing before transitioning to marketing, where she strictly enforces use of the Oxford comma. When not writing, she might be trying out new recipes, volunteering for more than she should, or playing with her dogs. She lives with her husband in their eventual dream house in Cleveland, Ohio, USA.

@rankin_writes

Infinite Possibilities

Michael Gardner

1

Adrian's name is typed across the front of the white envelope, but there's no address and no stamp. This was hand delivered.

He stands by his mailbox, raises a hand to shield his eyes from the sinking sun, peers up the road, turns and looks back down toward the corner. No one else is about. A couple of parrots chatter away as they fly overhead.

He lives in a neat suburban cul-de-sac. Quiet. New brick houses, middle class. Young trees not big enough to provide much shade. Tidy yards, except for number six. Adrian's not much of a gardener, but Candice refuses to be talked about like the owners of that house, so he gets out most weekends, mows, rakes, sprays for weeds. She takes care of the plants.

He looks back at the white envelope in his grease-stained hand. There's a small lump inside.

The sun is warm, bordering on hot, even though it's late in the day. He regrets his choice of tracksuit pants. His legs are sticky, moist beneath the material. A bead of sweat escapes his armpit, runs down his side. He blows hot air up across his nose and brow. It doesn't help.

He tears open the end of the envelope, upends the contents into his hand. A white USB. Unlabelled. Maybe a scam? he thinks. A virus? Malware?

But then why go to the trouble of finding out his name and where he lives? That seems very specific for a phishing scam. Why not just address the letter to the homeowner?

It's too hot, he thinks, wiping his brow. He trudges back to the house, the screen door screeching as he opens it.

It's five degrees cooler inside. The feel of the tiled floor beneath his bare feet is a pleasant relief. He moves down the hall, into the living/dining/kitchen space. It's modern, open, airy.

By the kitchen bench, he opens the bin, then hesitates with the USB in hand.

What did Candice say just the other night? Something about missing the old Adrian. The wild Adrian. He was hurt at the time. As if she'd expressed a desire to be with someone else. Someone he can't compete with. And the old Adrian *is* someone he can't compete with. The old Adrian exhausts him.

Still.

He closes the bin, tosses the USB next to his laptop on the bench. He'll decide later, he thinks.

Adrian was high and drunk when he met Candice.

It was late in the evening when his mates convinced him to try a new night club. It wasn't exactly his sort of place, but he relented, lined up, and forked out an exorbitant cover charge.

Inside was a dizzying assault of bass, lights, sweaty bodies, and the noise of people yelling at each other to be heard over the music. He soon gave up trying to talk to his friends, and they left him at the bar as they hit the dance floor.

Candice was dancing. He doesn't recall what she was wearing exactly, but he remembers her hair. Long, auburn, waves of movement that crashed around her. A halo of silk. He watched her move with abandon as he sipped his rum.

When she ceased whirling, when she turned and approached, he thought it was to him that she came. That's why he spoke. "Adrian."

Like his own name was a password that needed to be stated. Like it unlocked something special. And it did, kind of.

She smirked, veered at the last moment, sidled up next to him at the bar and signalled for the bartender. Then with her best Sylvester Stallone impression: "Adrian. Adrian. Addriannnnnn!"

He didn't know how to respond. She didn't let him. She ordered a couple of gin and tonics.

"Is one of them for me, Rocky?" he eventually asked.

She snorted a laugh, turned, looked him up and down. "No."

"Huh." He sipped again, swilled the liquid around his mouth. "You dance like a typhoon."

She regarded him quizzically. "Is that a good thing?"

"Absolutely. Ferocious. Unencumbered. Nature's force and power."

The bartender slid the drinks to Candice, took her cash, disappeared.

"Good answer," she said, smiling lopsidedly, genuinely. He remembered that through his booze haze. That lopsided smile. He used to get it a lot back then. "And how do you dance?" she asked. The bartender dropped her change on the alcohol sticky counter.

"I'm more like a sinking ship."

"So I'd engulf you?"

"If I'm lucky."

"You're not," she stated, picked up her drinks, and left without her change.

He watched her until she disappeared amongst the crowd, then he glanced at the coins on the bar. They glinted under the flashing lights. He felt like he'd missed something. Something that the alcohol wasn't quite letting him see, or feel. Something important, lost without him ever realising it was there in the first place.

But what was he going to do?

Later, as he stumbled from the bar, and along the wet street—had it rained? He couldn't remember—a taxi slowed next to him and the back window rolled down with an electric buzz.

"Yo, Adrian," came the mock deep voice, and there she was again, leaning out the window.

"You giving me a lift?" he asked, hopeful.

"Uh uh," she said, shaking her head. "You're off your tits, and I'm not that sort of girl."

"Oh." The scent of exhaust was acrid, like burnt plastic. It mixed with the smell of wet bitumen, forming a distinctive aroma that stayed with him long after. Two girlfriends were in the back with this lovely stranger. Two girlfriends giggling, urging her to leave him and close the window.

"I'll be back here next Saturday. Maybe if you bring me some of whatever you're on—"

"I'm not on anything," he lied, and received a disbelieving expression. He relented, shrugged, smiled. She smiled back.

"What then, Rocky?" he asked.

"Don't know. Maybe nothing. Maybe we dance. Let's see how it plays out."

"Next Saturday," he repeated.

She nodded, smiled, slapped the taxi door once on the side and it began to move. As it sped up, she leaned further out, and yelled, "Candice," then she was gone again, pulled back inside the cab by her two friends.

He's tinkering at his work bench in the garage when Candice returns home. He jumps a little as the automatic garage door starts to rise. It emits a mix of clunks and whirs, drowning out the hum of Candice's Corolla as it pulls into the drive, stops. It's dusk out, he sees, the streetlights just starting to warm up.

She steps out of the car, and his eyes are drawn to her legs, still shapely after all these years. She wears a pencil skirt, a white silk blouse. She looks unaffected by the heat. She looks stunning.

"Hi," he says, a grunt as much as a greeting. He refocusses on the dirty parts of the lawnmower carburettor lined up on his bench.

It's a familiar game they play. Distance, coolness. It's better than fighting. At least for him. Candice, she can get mad as hell, yell, and scream, then be over it an hour later. But Adrian holds onto things. Weighs each hurt, collects them until they overwhelm him.

"You didn't work today?" she says. Her tone is flat, neutral. No accusation there. Adrian senses one anyway.

"Rostered day off."

"Didn't you have one last week?"

He picks up the bowl nut, scrubs it with the wire brush. "They cut my shifts back," he says. He feels her watching him, but he refuses to look. She's very still. The street is quiet. If there weren't the whisking sound of the steel brush on the nut, he wonders if he'd hear anything.

He knows what she's thinking. She's thinking, 'I told you so.' When Action buses offered him an incentive to move to casual rates, he took it. More money, fewer shifts. But Candice was irate. Another bad career choice. Like when he dropped out of university and never went back. He sees that in her eyes as they dress for work each morning. Her in her suit, him in his blue uniform.

Finally, Candice moves. Her heels click as she glides across the concrete toward the door separating garage from house.

"I'm going out tonight," she tosses toward him casually, daring him to object. Once she would have asked him to join her, but not anymore. She's given up. Her work colleagues and friends just aren't his people. He's made that clear.

He says nothing. Just keeps cleaning. Candice disappears inside.

After he reassembles the lawnmower, he goes inside to the laundry and washes his hands in the tub. As he scrubs, he hears the automatic garage door closing. He knows he's missed Candice. Suspects she waited till he was cleaning up to leave.

It's been like this for a while. Since her mother died, yes, but probably even before that. Sometimes, Candice surprises Adrian with an offer of peace. Like taking him out to dinner a few weeks back where everything seemed easy, and for one evening it was relaxed between them, just like when they first met. But it was only one evening. Things reverted to normal as soon as he told her about moving to casual rates. She yelled, and he took it, and resented her once again for demanding such a huge say in his life while she excluded him from her decisions. Like when she unilaterally chose to abandon their efforts at a family.

Her car turns over, whines as it reverses out onto the street, then gurgles as she drives away. He listens until the sound fades. He sighs, dries his hands.

Back in the kitchen, on his way to the fridge, he spies his computer and the USB lying next to it. He stops, wonders. Maybe if he's careful he can take a quick peek. He'll disconnect the wifi, avoid execute files. Maybe if he does that there will be no risk of infection. Not that he really knows, but he's curious, and he's working hard to justify opening it up.

"Fuck it," he says. He pulls out one of the kitchen stools, sits at the bench. He starts up the computer, sticks the USB in the drive.

There's one file. A video file. Can a video file contain malware? He doesn't know. Probably. He runs his antivirus software, it comes up clean. He opens the file.

A widescreen shot of a drover's hut. It's made of old, grey wood, solidly built. The sort of cabin he'd expect to find in the middle of a national park, but this one is set on a large block of cleared land, a modern road in the foreground, paddocks surrounding it filled with yellow flowers that he suspects are canola. In the distance, movement. Maybe sheep grazing? He can't quite tell. He watches for a while. Nothing changes. He thinks the hut is enclosed by fencing, but the camera shot is not close and it's difficult to tell.

It takes him a while to realise the video is not silent. There's a low drone, like traffic, but a long way away. He increases the volume, and it comes a little stronger, but he can't place exactly what it is. Occasionally, the drone is usurped by a short song from a bird offscreen. But never for long. Soon enough, that hum is back. And all the while the shot of the hut remains the same. Nothing changes. Nothing happens.

Impatient, he scrolls further forward in the video, moving halfway in. Still no change. Just the hut, the paddocks, the empty black road, the drone. He skips to the end. One hour and thirteen minutes and it's the same scene. Although perhaps the day is a little brighter, a result of the sun rising slowly.

He closes the video, stares at his computer screen, unsure what to make of it. He can't imagine why someone would leave this for him, or what he's supposed to do with it.

He runs the antivirus program again. Nothing. He sighs, closes the laptop, then orders takeout without checking the fridge.

He doesn't hear Candice come in. His laptop is connected to the flat screen television in the lounge room. Adrian sits close, on the soft carpet, peering up. He's about halfway through the video, the fifth time he's watched it. He's staring intently at the small window on the left side of the hut. It's covered by a lace curtain, but soon a shadow will pass behind it. Yes, there.

"What are you watching?" Candice asks. Her words sound dull, diluted, like he's sitting at the bottom of a pool looking up at people talking on the deck.

"Huh," he says, turning to find her standing at the edge of the room in a black dress, her hair tied back, a little eyeshadow, lipstick, no wedding band. He glances back at the screen, and the cabin. The shadow is gone.

He feels like he was on the verge of understanding something. That he could nearly see over the crest, but now it's gone. He blinks. His eyes are sore.

"Someone sent me this video in the mail," he says, as if that explains things.

"Who?" Candice asks. She moves into the room, tosses her handbag onto the coffee table. The thud of it makes Adrian jump. He closes his eyes, enjoys the momentary relief it provides. Opens them, glances at the screen, then Candice.

"Don't know. It was anonymous. But the envelope had my name on it, and this USB inside." He gestures to the laptop, his eyes finding the small white protrusion from its side. He realises how silly it sounds. He expects admonishment, but he should know by now that Candice doesn't do predictable.

"Ooh, I read about something like this on Facebook," she says. She sits next to him, folds her legs to the side, props on an outstretched arm. It's the closest they've been for a while. He can't help but smell her—lavender soap, a dash of

musky   perfume,   something   else.
Aftershave? Sweat? He frowns.

"Facebook?" he says. There's more he
wants to say, to ask, but words escape
him.

"Yeah, it's a game. Friends nominate
you, and this company sends out these
videos. You're supposed to work it out."

"Work what out?" he asks, glancing at
the screen. This close it looks pixelated,
grainy. The drone from the video is
prevalent, setting his teeth on edge.

"I don't know exactly. If I did, it
wouldn't be as fun, would it? Maybe
where this cabin is, what's important
about it? It might be like geocaching. You
know, follow the coordinates, find the
treasure, take something to prove you
found it, leave something for the next
person."

"Oh." The shot has definitely gotten
brighter and the shadows shorter. Like
the sun is directly overhead. Here comes
the bird again, wait, yes there. A warble. A
measure of music, then silence. "Who'd
sign me up for this?"

Candice laughs. "I would have done it if
I'd thought of it. This could be good for
you. Get you out of the house. You're
always stuck in that garage."

He swallows, looks at her watching the TV screen.

"Okay, I need a shower, then I'm going to bed. I've got an early meeting tomorrow," she says.

She places a hand on his shoulder, pushes as she rises to her feet. She kisses him on the top of his head, then disappears from the room and heads toward the back of the house.

She didn't say anything about her night, he realises. She has a knack of asking questions, and yet she gives away very little nowadays. Maybe it's always been like this. Maybe he doesn't know much about her at all. Only what she wants him to know.

He stops the video, stares at the blank TV screen. Candice encouraging him to keep going has suddenly put a damper on the exercise. And yet he doesn't want to go to bed. Not yet. He'd prefer to slip into the sheets when Candice is asleep. Like he has most nights since her mother died.

It's part guilt, part anger that she never talked to him after, that she sank into herself for so long before reappearing as if nothing had changed. Even though she did change. She decided to stop trying for a family. She didn't even ask him if that was okay.

He's afraid if he says anything about how much that hurt, it'll lead to them both telling each other what they really feel. That he'll say the words he'll never be able to take back. He doesn't want that. Doesn't want to risk it all ending. So, he avoids her instead.

He finds himself replaying the video, starting from the beginning again.

They'd been going out for a couple of weeks when they ended up parked down by the main beach late one night (or was it early one morning?) smoking weed in his ancient Ford Escort. Windows down, sea breeze rustling their hair. He was captivated by hers, which undulated like the dark waves he couldn't see, but could hear, and that he imagined were pounding the sand relentlessly somewhere in that darkness beyond his front windshield.

He was too stoned to drive. He might have said something to that effect, because she offered. Demanded it, even. Like it was a dare.

"Nuh, you'll wreck my pride and joy," he'd said, grinning around the blunt. He suddenly wondered what he'd do if a cop rolled by and shone a torch on the rust bucket with the windows down, smoke wafting out.

"Come on, don't be a wuss." She liked to needle him. He liked to let her. A vaccination from boredom.

He passed her the last of the joint, and she sucked it down to the nib, the flame glowing orange in the dark, lighting just enough of her lips for him to imagine kissing her again.

She tossed the butt, held the smoke in her lungs, motioned for the keys. He relented. Searched his pockets for them, couldn't find them. Looked on the floor. She exhaled with a rush, coughed, regained composure.

"They're in the ignition, you half-baked fuckwit," she said, laughing. His eyes fell to the steering column, saw the glint of metal. He laughed too.

"Come on. Scooch."

"You'll be careful?" he asked.

"Hell no," she said. The look in her eyes both excited and terrified him. He opened the door, got out and circled around the back as she slid across the console into the driver's seat.

He'd barely got his seatbelt on when she jammed the car into reverse and gunned it backward, braking late.

"Jesus," he yelped.

"Oh, you ain't seen nothing yet." She put it in drive, hit the accelerator.

The car wasn't powerful, but she extracted all of what it had, careering up and down hilly streets, the wind rushing inside, her manic laughter surrounding him. He held onto the dash, white fingertips boring marks into the vinyl.

He must have told her to slow down twenty times, moving from requests to pleading. She didn't listen.

At some point, the car rocketed past the city limits, down a road he didn't know, trees close and leaning in. The weak lights on his car did little to illuminate the dark countryside.

"Candice, stop. Stop now," he ordered. She didn't listen. Just kept going. "Now, or I stop us. This is crazy," he implored. She never even glanced at him, just kept grinning, driving into the dark tunnel of trees.

He later blamed the pot for the rash decision. She did too. But there was something else there too. He didn't like losing control.

He wrenched hard on the parking brake.

The car screamed; Candice might have as well. The back tyres locked and sent smoke into the air, as the car fishtailed across the bitumen. It must have put Candice off her game because at the last moment she jerked the wheel, and the car spun, slid off the road, and ended up facing back the way they'd come. They'd been lucky. It had pulled up a few feet shy of a large gum tree, angled up on an embankment. Adrian could smell sap, eucalyptus, burnt rubber.

In the aftermath, the world was silent outside, harsh breathing inside. Candice still gripped the wheel tightly, hunched, staring out the windscreen into the sickly yellow beams of the headlights.

She turned slowly, looked at him. He felt his face grow hot. He shrugged, his effort at an apology.

"You crazy son of a bitch," she said, so quietly he almost didn't hear her. To his surprise she grabbed his shirt and pulled him hard into a kiss. Then her hands were on his chest, his stomach, undoing the zip of his pants.

He knew that, whatever this was, it was dangerous. He let it happen anyway.

He tells himself he no longer needs Candice's approval, but he's not sure that's true. Would he have really volunteered to take the new number thirty-three bus route if she hadn't judged him the other day? Passively of course, nothing said directly. But he had a toe in the water, felt the temperature change, and now he's reacted.

No one else wanted the route because it meanders through the new estates on the outskirts of the city. Which are a long way from his home, and the depot. A long way from everything, really. Nevertheless, he finds the drive pleasant.

This far out, most people use cars, so passengers are few, and mostly polite elderly people making trips to the shops. The bus is new. It has that new-car smell, laced with a hint of diesel. It's cool, the air conditioner cranked high.

The bus groans as he slows for a roundabout (they're everywhere in these new suburbs). He leans in his seat as he swings out onto it. The bus roars as he exits, as he accelerates again, moves up through the gears.

His only passenger hits the stop button, which dings, and he drifts to a stop beside the next bus shelter. The old man steps off. No one boards. He drives the empty bus away.

He turns onto Peterman Drive, which runs along the edge of the new estates. A long, double lane road with half-built houses on the left, and paddocks marked for future subdivision on the right. He speeds up to 80, the limit out here, enjoys the feel of the heavy machine powering over the bitumen.

That's when he sees it: the hut from the USB, alone amongst a field of yellow canola.

A cool sweat emerges upon his forehead. He feels weak, and anxious. He can't help but stop.

He doesn't screech on the brakes or swing the steering wheel wildly; he's an experienced bus driver. He checks his mirrors, signals, pulls to the left, gently riding the brakes until he rolls to a smooth stop. The doors open with a hiss, hot air spilling into the cab momentarily neutralising the effects of the air conditioner. He sits in his seat for a beat, thinking, then he puts the hazard lights on, jumps out.

He walks around the back of the bus. A burst of hot air rushes over him as a car races by. Then it's just him, the bus still idling, gurgling away, and the hut in the middle of the paddock.

It's a couple of hundred metres back from the road, surrounded by a high, chain-link fence. Weeds have grown up around it, a few stray canola plants mixed in. There're no power lines, no telephone lines. The hut doesn't look like it belongs in its current location. It must have been moved. He wonders if it has heritage status. That might explain the fencing.

He removes his phone, takes a couple of photos, then, on a whim, he records a short video. About thirty seconds. When he's done, he plays it back. It's the sound that strikes him. The sound of his bus. It comes through his phone speakers tinny, small, but so familiar it sets the hairs on his arms on end. The gurgle of his bus through his phone sounds like the low drone that soundtracks the video on the USB.

He swallows, appraises the hut again. He glances at the bus, at his phone, sees the time. He's been here ten minutes. He'll be in the shit if he doesn't get back on his route soon.

He takes one last look, puts his phone away and climbs back on board. He's suddenly certain he's not alone, that a passenger, way up back, has been watching him. He glances in the mirror hurriedly, but there's no one there. He shudders, checks his side mirrors, eases the bus back out onto the road. As he drives, he can't shake the feeling that he's being watched.

Adrian sits at the kitchen bench, hunched over his computer. He doesn't realise Candice is close until he feels her hand caress his shoulder. He jerks upright, feels her breath against his cheek.

"This again. It's really got you in, hasn't it? Any luck?"

He half turns, and she's right there. He can smell her, feel her warmth. If she notices his discomfort, she doesn't let on. She's focussed on the video.

"This isn't from the USB. I took it this afternoon with my phone," he says.

"Your phone?" She turns toward him. They're close. Their lips barely a couple of inches apart. An instinct directs him to close the distance, kiss her. Another makes him turn away. He looks at the screen again without really seeing it. His other senses are focussed on her, where his eyes want to be. Her heat, the feel of her hand resting on his shoulder, the scent of lavender soap, the soft sound of her breathing. He doesn't know why she makes him nervous these days. He's a school kid with a first crush. A girl he likes, but says he doesn't.

"I'm driving a new route—"

"Really," she interrupts. "Good for you." She doesn't seem afflicted with his hesitancy. She kisses him on the cheek, casually throws an arm around him. He tries not to recoil—they've barely touched in God knows how long. His fault, mostly. Because he's worried he's not good enough. Because he didn't live up to her expectations. Because he stopped her seeing her dying mother and how do you forgive something like that? He's punishing himself, he knows. But if he doesn't, wouldn't she?

"It's out on the other side of the city where Sunder Estates is going up. Right toward the backend of the route, I find this hut. I had to stop and take a couple of shots."

"And a video."

"Yeah."

She releases him, sits on the stool next to him, leans into his space to get a closer look. The video is paused, but she hits play. He watches with her. The hut. His eyes focus on the left window. He wonders if she sees it. The subtle movement in the curtain. Not brushed aside, but pressed, like someone has leaned on it, pushed it up against the window. And all the while there's the gurgling drone of his idling bus, transformed somehow into something that burrows into his teeth.

"It looks so similar to what you were watching the other night."

And sounds the same, he thinks, but doesn't say.

"Did you go in? What's inside?" she asks.

"I was working. I couldn't." He glances at her and is pleased when she doesn't shoot him a disapproving glare.

"Okay. Well, when are we going to check it out?" she asks, regarding him with a cocked eyebrow and a smirk.

"We?"

"Why not? Can't let you have all the fun."

He suddenly feels young again. An adventure. They used to go everywhere together and say it was an adventure. Even when it wasn't. Shopping. The beach. A day trip to nowhere. A weekend away. She made it adventurous. She'd make something up, do something stupid, bring along some dope or grog, and he enjoyed it, mostly. And the little part of him that didn't, the times she made him nervous or fearful, well, he felt alive, at least. Unlike this novocaine existence he's leading now.

"Okay. Yes," he says, like he's just made up his mind. "Let's do it together. Find out what the hell this thing is all about. How about tomorrow?"

She makes a clicking sound with her tongue and teeth. An 'I'd like to but can't', sound, and instantly he feels the adrenaline leak from his system, his shoulders slump.

"Tomorrow is packed with client meetings," she says.

"I understand," he jumps in quickly. "They're more important." Always are, he thinks. "Maybe some other time."

The short video has ended. He reaches out and closes the laptop, rises from the stool.

"Where are you going?"

"Garage," he says. He sees that she knows that he's getting up to leave her. To be by himself, where he can keep his hands and mind busy over nothing important.

"Fuck it," she says stopping him. He looks back. "No, I'm in. I'll blow off my four o'clock appointment. But be ready to go as soon as I get home, okay? I want to check it out before it gets dark."

He finds himself grinning like a kid who's been told it's Christmas tomorrow. He nods. "Four it is."

They went to Thailand after Candice graduated. A last hurrah before she started work as an accountant.

Ostensibly, he was still studying, but he couldn't settle. He moved through a variety of unrelated subjects hoping something would stick. He quite enjoyed astrophysics, but Candice convinced him there was no future in it. So, he enrolled in marketing. A future she could see herself in when they got back to Australia.

For the first week in Thailand, they holed up in a backpacker dive on Khao San Road, Bangkok. Each day seemed hotter than the last. Smog and sweat, the stench of baked bitumen, exhaust, and ripe, tropical fruit. Head in a constant haze, hungover from the night before, the smell of alcohol sweating from his pores. Of a night they'd walk the strip, drink and eat at little plastic tables that appeared on the street at dusk. Drink some more.

They'd find somewhere to dance, make chit chat with fellow backpackers, drink. Finish the night with a feed of cheap street food, a bottle of water from the 24 hour Seven Eleven, fuck, pass out.

On the second to last day in Bangkok, they spent the day on the roof of the hostel. There was a pool up there, umbrellas, an outdoor bar. It was no tropical oasis. Mostly baking cement, thick smog that obscured the view of the city. The pool water was more soup warm than refreshing.

They were both laying on deck chairs, two large bottles of Singha beer on the table between them. Candice might have been reading something, but he wasn't.

He was staring up into that half gloom that obscured the sun. A shadow passed over him, and when he looked, he found a pale, red headed girl looking at them both.

"Hi," she said, an Australian accent. "This seat taken?" she asked, gesturing to the empty chair beside Candice.

"Nope, all yours," Candice answered, looking up from her book.

"Thanks so much," she said. She spread a towel over the hot plastic surface, then lay down. She removed a cotton top to expose green swimmers and freckled, white skin. "My boyfriend and I just got in, and I'm excited. You guys been here long?" she asked. She began to lather sunscreen on her arms and neck. Adrian didn't really want to chat. He felt like shit from the night before, hence the beer. His thinking was that if he could get drunk again, his body would be tricked into forgetting his hangover.

"Nearly a week," Candice said. She placed her book face down. "We're heading to Ko Tao tomorrow evening. We're going to do some diving."

"That sounds amazing," the girl said, genuine excitement in her voice. "I haven't heard of Ko Tao. Is it nice?"

"Hope so," Candice responded. She hesitated, then rose a little and extended a hand. "I'm Candice, and this is my partner, Adrian."

Adrian took the signal, half rose, waved. "Hey," he mumbled, before slumping back onto his chair.

"Nice to meet you both. I'm Taylor."

Taylor and Candice quickly eased into a conversation as if they'd known each other for years. Adrian was glad they didn't try to involve him. He followed for a little while, but then allowed their words to dissolve into meaningless sounds. They washed over him like waves until he dozed in the chair.

When he woke it was dusk, and there was a big guy perched on the end of Taylor's deck chair. Tall, well built, crewcut, like an army brat.

"Rise and shine," Candice said. "This is Mike."

Adrian reached for his beer, took a sip, found it hot. Mike leaned across Candice, extended a meaty hand. Adrian took it, uncomfortable with the way he veered into Candice's space, skin touching skin.

"Hey," Adrian said, pumping his hand once, releasing him. He was glad to watch Mike pull away from Candice again.

"Mike and Taylor were going to check out Soi Cowboy. Want to go?"

Adrian snorted a laugh. "The stripper district?"

"Yeah, it'll be fun," Candice said.

Adrian didn't think it sounded much fun. It sounded odd. But he wasn't going to argue in front of Candice's new friends. "I guess," he said.

When they went later that evening, he was surprised to find it wasn't as bad as he thought it would be. Mike ended up being pretty decent. The bar they chose was topless, but it was too early in the evening for any of the crazy shit that Adrian was worried would make everyone feel uncomfortable. And most importantly, the place was air conditioned, which was a huge relief after six days of suffocating heat.

Out on the streets he'd seen and fed a baby elephant. With traditional music blaring from speakers around him, he'd bought bananas from the handler. He couldn't help but wonder if the elephant was maltreated. Probably. And he felt guilty. Yet he enjoyed giving them to the calf, hoping they provided some joy for it, at least in that moment.

Candice sidled up to him, drawing his attention from Mike, who'd been talking about football.

"You having fun?"

"Yeah," he said, grinning. "I am, actually. They're nice people. Sorry about earlier, I—"

"Was hungover, I understand. We're all good now, right?"

"Of course."

"You know I love you," she whispered, and while it wasn't the first time she'd said it, it made him tingle in his belly, his chest, his balls.

"I love you too," he said, leaning in. She kissed him on the cheek, then the mouth, pulled back, leaned into his ear again.

"Taylor suggested we swap partners tonight. What do you think?"

Adrian jerked back like he'd been slapped. He felt a smirk on his lips, but then it fell as he saw the serious look on Candice's face. He glanced at Mike, his arm around Taylor, watching him and Candice. They were waiting for him, he saw.

"What? I..." His head was spinning. He licked his lips, but couldn't seem to wet them. He felt trapped, lost. He suddenly wanted to go home.

Candice draped two arms around his neck, pulled him close. "We don't have to," she whispered into his ear. "Of course we don't. But... I've never done anything like that. I don't think you have either. We're young. We have our whole lives together..." she left the thought hanging.

He regarded Taylor again. It was like he was seeing her through fresh eyes. She was attractive, in her way. Lithe, athletic. Yet did that matter? He didn't know. He looked at Mike. He didn't like the thought of that huge body held up over Candice.

"You can say no," she said, as if reading his mind. "I won't mind."

But was that true?

Before he could answer, the bargirl arrived with the tequila shots Mike had ordered. He grabbed one quickly and threw it back, grimacing as it burned his throat.

"And after?" he said.

"After, we go back to normal. This is an overseas thing. A Thailand thing."

"What stays in Thailand," he muttered, and she chuckled, nodded. He sighed. "I'll need a few more of these," he said, holding up the empty shot glass, waggling it.

She kissed him again. Long, passionate. But he felt something leak from him. Something he wasn't sure he'd get back.

He sits in the passenger seat staring out the window as the city falls away behind them. He knows where to go, but Candice insists on following the GPS.

He wonders who all of these people are that have decided to pitch houses on flat ground miles from the city. He realises his house was probably like this once. Until suburbs grew around it, leaving him feeling entitled to judge others who had to settle further out.

The car slows, and he shakes himself from his stupor. Candice has turned onto Peterman Drive, houses on the left, paddocks on the right. She accelerates, and soon he sees the cabin nestled amongst the canola crop, the chain link fence around it.

He looked up cabins like this on his computer and found a number of images of huts in the snowy mountains. Alpine cabins used by drovers, or people who'd become lost. A shared, public resource.

Temporary protection against cold winter nights, death.

Perhaps this cabin was the same, once. Its odd location only because the forest that once surrounded it has long been cleared, the surrounding country terraformed into arable land. Now, even that has been encroached upon by suburban sprawl.

Gravel crunches under the wheels of the car as Candice eases onto the verge. Adrian feels the seatbelt grip his chest as Candice brakes more harshly than she intended. She cuts the engine, silencing the tick, tick, tick of the indicator and the buzz of the engine. It's abruptly silent. Invasively quiet. Not another car to be seen or heard on this stretch of new road that looks designed for back-to-back traffic. Future planning at work, Adrian thinks.

"Well," Candice says, the edge of her lips turned up in an excited smile. "What now?"

If he's honest, he hasn't thought that through. That chain link fence looks larger than he remembers. "I guess we go check it out."

They exit the car, check the road for non-existent traffic, cross together. Adrian notices a chorus of buzzing that he presumes is locusts in the canola plants.

The first hurdle is easy enough. A wire fence set a few metres back from the road. Star pickets and three strands of wire. He pulls the top wire up taut so that Candice can duck, and slide through the gap he's made. Then he pushes the same wire down hard, so he can step over it and onto the uneven ground of the paddock. There are depressions in the ground like livestock trod through here recently. Depressions hidden amongst the vibrant green plants, the golden canola flowers.

"Watch your step," he says, as he leads the way, pushing a path through the flora, trying not to crush too much of the crop.

It doesn't take long to reach the chain link fence. He places a hand on it, clawing his fingers through the hexagonal holes. He glances back the way he's come, sees Candice with eyes downcast on the path ahead, sees the thin trail they've cut through the canola. It's obvious that they are the first people to come out to this cabin in a while, at least since the crop matured. It makes him wonder if the maker of the video wanted him to come out here after all.

Candice catches up, places a hand on his shoulder. "How do we get in?"

He doesn't know, so he doesn't reply. He should have brought some pliers to cut the fence. Although would he have done that? That's surely a crime. He spies a gate along the east side, points. "Maybe we try that."

"Good work, Sherlock," Candice says. She goes past him toward the gate.

Adrian hesitates, surveys the rest of the boundary. He wonders again about the fence. If this were a heritage site, shouldn't it have a sign? Something advising of the significance of this construction, why it is being protected, how it is being restored? But he sees nothing like that. He shakes the thought, follows Candice.

The gate is chained, padlocked. But when he rattles it, he sees that there is plenty of flex. He pushes until the gate strains against the chain, and Candice gives a little joyous yelp as she drops to hands and knees and, awkwardly, squeezes through the gap at the bottom. Once through, she holds the gate for him. It's a tighter fit for him. A stray piece of wire tears his shirt and draws blood from his arm, but he gets through.

Candice moves toward the front door. Adrian glances back at the road, checks they are alone. They are. No cars in sight, no people. Yet he feels watched. He surveys the hut, no cameras. He's just on edge about trespassing, he thinks. He follows Candice up onto the porch where she waits by the door.

"Shall I do the honours?" she asks. "Or you?"

"You do it," he says. He expects it to be locked, but the old, rusted, metal handle turns smoothly, and the wooden door swings open silently. A waft of stale air hits him. A smell of wood, and dust.

It's darker inside, cooler. It takes a few seconds for Adrian's eyes to adjust. He steps over the threshold.

It's small, one room, and oddly furnished. Adrian's eyes are drawn to the faded pink recliner sitting on a modern, floral rug. An old, portable television, rabbit ears akimbo, is set on a high table in front of the chair. There's something odd about the TV. There's a weird silver box attached to the left side, which looks homemade.

Next to the recliner is a side table, a book set on top at an odd angle, as if someone tossed it there casually after reading.

The rest of the room is more predictable. On the far side is a wood stove made of thick, black metal, and a small woodpile. There's a kitchen bench and metal sink nearby, and a table made from an old, thick stump. On the right, pressed up against the wall, a single bed frame, no mattress, springs rusted.

"Wow," Candice says quietly as she eases past Adrian and moves to the kitchenette. She squats down and opens the stove, which squeaks.

Adrian's eyes are drawn to the recliner, to the television. He moves closer, appraises the book on the table: *Infinite Possibilities: Navigating the Multiverse*. A glance toward Candice shows her still investigating the kitchen. He slumps into the recliner, picks up the book.

There's a clicking sound. He looks up to see the television warming up. The screen clarifies into an image of a person's head and neck. A very familiar head and neck. His head and neck.

Adrian's heart beats harder, and he feels a sensation in his bowels like someone squeezing. He feels like he's falling.

The man on the screen is not exactly like him, he realises. This version wears glasses, is a little thicker around the neck, a little greyer at the temples. And yet the resemblance is uncanny. It's like staring long and hard at your own reflection in the mirror until you begin to really take in the details of your skin, until familiar images begin to appear strange.

Other Adrian, he thinks.

Other Adrian opens his mouth to speak, but then Candice drops an old frypan, which clangs loudly. Other Adrian's eyes behind the thick glasses dart somewhere to Adrian's left as if he can, impossibly, see into this room. As if he has just heard that clang, and has noticed Candice.

Other Adrian looks back at Adrian, scowls, shakes his head ever so slightly, then the image is gone, the screen black again.

Adrian can't move. He stares at the blank screen, can just make out a distorted reflection of himself. He tries to rationalise what he just saw, but can't. It's like when he was a kid and took apart his watch to understand how it worked, but couldn't put it back together again.

He jumps when Candice touches his shoulder. "Are you just chilling out or something?" she says, snorting a laugh. "Find any clues?"

Clues? He's not sure. He found something. "Did you..." he points at the television.

"What?"

"You didn't..." he tries again, still staring at the blank screen. "I saw... I found..."

"What?" she says, confused. He understands that she missed it.

He recalls Other Adrian scowling, the shake of the head, and intuits that the image wasn't meant for her. He did something wrong bringing her here. Perhaps he did something wrong in coming here himself. He tears his eyes from the screen, glances at the book he's holding. It feels heavy in his hands.

Candice takes it from him, looks at it. A smile slowly materialises on her face. "This is neat," she says. "Your next clue, I'd say."

"A clue?"

"You didn't notice?"

"What?"

She holds the book out toward him. He reads the title again. He doesn't understand. His face bunches, and he sees that Candice sees he isn't following.

"You're focusing on the wrong thing," she says, pointing toward the bottom of the book cover. "Apparently, this book was written by you."

"Infinite Possibilities" continues in next month's issue.
See part I of Michael Gardner's story "Infinite Possibilities" online at Metaphorosis.
If you liked it, leave a comment. Authors love that!
Remember to subscribe to our e-mail updates so you'll know when new stories are posted.

About the story

Before I wrote "Infinite Possibilities", I'd read a horror short story that told its tale by describing a series of strange videos. While horror involving videos or photos is not new, I thought the way the story had been done was quite fresh. It was set up as a weird, ambiguous mystery. That got me thinking of my own mystery video, and at some point, I settled on the idea that it should be of an old cabin, like those sometimes found in Australia's alpine state forests.

I'm not quite sure when I decided to mix the cabin video with parallel worlds. But my mind does wander to the idea of parallel worlds often, usually to wonder about what unexpected, horrible things they might contain. For this story, I began to like the idea of my protagonist, Adrian, discovering multiple worlds that contained multiple versions of himself—many like him, but some that had ulterior motives.

The part of the story that evolved most as I wrote was the relationship between Candice and Adrian. I didn't start off thinking their relationship would be strained. In fact, close to the first thing I wrote was their first meeting at the night club. I think that scene could just have easily led to a couple that doted on each other and never had any issues. However, something about the scene made me think these people were opposites, which clearly led to the spark between them, but also conflict. This showed up more and more in the story as I went.

This novella is the longest story I've ever written. It merged two ideas that I thought were interesting, but weird, and a couple of characters I really came to love. I'm glad it found a home with Metaphorosis.

A question for the author

Q: What tools do you write with?

A: The obvious tools are my laptop and Microsoft Word. I'm not much of a pen and paper person. For starters, my handwriting is atrocious, so I often can't read what I've written a few days later.

I'm also not much of a plotter. I've met a few plotters recently and have been impressed with the tools they use. Scrivener for detailed outlining and planning, spreadsheets, multiple character summaries, scene descriptions, etc. It's not that I don't plan at all, but it's mostly done in my head. A key concept, an idea of the ending, a character or two. When I have attempted to write down plans or character descriptions in the past, I find I'm writing the story. So, I tend to just keep going and write it.

The downside of being a pantser is I do multiple, extensive edits and re-writes of my first drafts. Well, some might call it a downside, but I weirdly enjoy editing. Add in a bit of internet research, draw on some lived experiences, a grammar and spell check, and that's about it for my writing tools.

About the author

Michael Gardner is a writer of fantasy and horror who masquerades as an economist by day. His work has appeared in *Writers of the Future Volume 36, Aurealis, Bourbon Penn,* and *Metaphorosis*. He is also a three-time finalist for the Aurealis Awards. You can find out more about Michael and his work at: www.michael-s-gardner.com

Copyright

Title information

Metaphorosis September 2022

ISSN: 2573-136X (online)
ISBN: 978-1-64076-236-7 (e-book)
ISBN: 978-1-64076-237-4 (paperback)

Copyright

Publisher

Metaphorosis
a magazine of speculative fiction

Metaphorosis Magazine is an imprint of
Metaphorosis Publishing
Neskowin, OR, USA

Discounts available

Substantial discounts are available for educational institutions, including writing workshops. Discounts are also available for quantity purchases. For details, contact Metaphorosis at metaphorosis.com/about

Metaphorosis Publishing

Metaphorosis offers beautifully written science fiction and fantasy. Our imprints include:

Metaphorosis Magazine
Plant Based Press
Verdage
Vestige

You can also find us:
@MetaphorosisMag, @Metaphorosis
www.facebook.com/metaphorosis

Help keep Metaphorosis running by supporting us at
Patreon.com/metaphorosis

See more about some of our books on the following pages.

Metaphorosis

a magazine of speculative fiction

Metaphorosis is an online speculative fiction magazine dedicated to quality writing. We publish an original story every week, along with author bios, interviews, and notes on story origins.

We also publish monthly print and e-book issues, as well as yearly Best of and Complete anthologies.

Come and see us online at magazine.Metaphorosis.com.

Plant Based Press

plant
based
press

Vegan-friendly science fiction and fantasy, including anthologies of the year's best SFF stories, from 2016-2020.

Chambers of the Heart
speculative stories
by
B. Morris Allen

A heart that's a building, a dog that's a program, a woman sinking irretrievably — stories about love, loss, and movement.

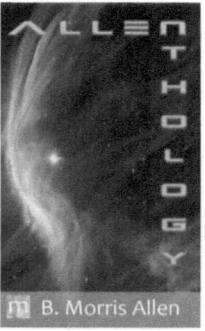

Susurrus

A darkly romantic story of magic, love, and suffering.

Allenthology: Volume I

Including three full collections of SFF stories.

Verdage

Science fiction and fantasy books for writers – full of great stories, often with an additional focus on the craft of speculative fiction writing.

Reading 5X5 x3

Changes

How do stories move from 'maybe' to published?

Here are 15 case studies of stories published in *Metaphorosis* magazine.

Reading 5X5 x2

Duets

How do authors' voices change when they collaborate?

A round-robin of five talented science fiction and fantasy authors collaborating with each other and writing solo.

Including stories by Evan Marcroft, David Gallay, J. Tynan Burke, L'Erin Ogle, and Douglas Anstruther.

Score

an SFF symphony

An anthology with an emotional score from the heights of joy to the depths of despair – but always with a little hope shining through.

Reading 5X5

Five stories, five times

See how different writers take on the same material.

Reading 5X5

Writers' Edition

Two extra stories, the story seed, and authors' notes on writing.

Vestige

Novelettes, novellas, and novels by Metaphorosis authors.

The Nocturnals
Mariah Montoya

Night is Dangerous. Day is deadly.

Where day and night last thirty years, humans move constantly stay ahead of the night and cruel Nocturnals that call it home. But a boy is lost out there.

www.ingramcontent.com/pod-product-compliance
Lightning Source LLC
Chambersburg PA
CBHW020639110726
47899CB00002B/821

* 9 7 8 1 6 4 0 7 6 2 3 7 4 *